The First Kiss

I rode the wave all the way to shore until the board bottomed out on sand and I fell off. I whipped around and found Cade in the water pumping the air with both his fists.

"Awesome!" he yelled as he swam toward me. He came up right beside me, grabbed me up in a huge hug, and swung me around. "That was great for a first time," he said.

As he put me down on the sand I looked up at him, grinning. He looked down at me and suddenly everything stopped. I looked in his eyes as he leaned into me and then I felt his lips on mine.

Gwenny always talked about a "wow factor," and I instantly felt that. I leaned into him as he deepened the kiss, feeling the whole world fall away, like we were the only two people existing.

The Summer My Life Began

SHANNON GREENLAND

speak
An Imprint of Penguin Group (USA) Inc.

SPEAK

Published by the Penguin Group

Penguin Group (USA) Inc., 345 Hudson Street, New York, New York 10014, U.S.A.
Penguin Group (Canada), 90 Eglinton Avenue East, Suite 700, Toronto, Ontario, Canada M4P 2Y3
(a division of Pearson Penguin Canada Inc.)
Penguin Books Ltd, 80 Strand, London WC2R 0RL, England
Penguin Ireland, 25 St Stephen's Green, Dublin 2, Ireland (a division of Penguin Books Ltd)
Penguin Group (Australia), 250 Camberwell Road, Camberwell, Victoria 3124, Australia
(a division of Pearson Australia Group Pty Ltd)
Penguin Books India Pvt Ltd, 11 Community Centre, Panchsheel Park, New Delhi - 110 017, India
Penguin Group (NZ), 67 Apollo Drive, Rosedale, Auckland 0632, New Zealand
(a division of Pearson New Zealand Ltd.)
Penguin Books (South Africa) (Pty) Ltd, 24 Sturdee Avenue,
Rosebank, Johannesburg 2196, South Africa

Registered Offices: Penguin Books Ltd, 80 Strand, London WC2R 0RL, England

Published by Speak, an imprint of Penguin Group (USA) Inc., 2012

1 3 5 7 9 10 8 6 4 2

Copyright © Shannon Greenland, 2012
All rights reserved

LIBRARY OF CONGRESS CATALOGING-IN-PUBLICATION DATA IS AVAILABLE

Speak ISBN 978-0-14-241347-0

Design by Irene Vandervoort
Text set in ITC Esprit

Printed in the United States of America

ALWAYS LEARNING   PEARSON

For all my wonderful readers . . .

The Summer
My Life Began

Chapter One

My sister and I had heard the same things our whole lives. An Ivy League education was expected. Medicine and law were the only two career options. We should marry rich from the most prestigious families.

I cringe when I think about the ridiculous standards. My parents were status seekers, plain and simple. And all my friends lived the exact same lifestyle. Fancy houses, prep schools, expensive clothes, trips to Paris at a moment's notice. Our whole lives were mapped out for us.

And for the most part, none of my friends seemed bothered by it. Why would they be? They were fine going to Harvard, Yale, Dartmouth, wherever. They were fine marrying who their parents told them to. They were fine going into the family business. They were just plain *fine*.

And I guess I was fine too. I didn't know any different. I liked pleasing my parents and tried to be the daughter I knew they expected me to be. I liked succeeding, having them proud of me. I embraced the whole "need to have a goal" thing, and I knew what it took to get to where I wanted. I wasn't valedictorian for nothing.

But over this last year, my senior year of high school, I started feeling like I was missing something. Like even though I had everything, there was so much *more* out there. I chalked it up to being nervous about graduating and starting college.

And now it is the end of May, and I will be starting my freshman year of college in a few months. I am about to go down a path that has been planned for me probably since my conception: Ivy League university, then law school, and then a position at my dad's firm. But now that it's actually happening, I have no desire to do any of it. I know there is more out there for me, I just don't know what.

"Hey, Em." Gwyneth, my younger sister, plopped down beside me on the couch.

I glanced up from where I was supposed to be studying for my AP history final.

"This came for you." My sister flicked an envelope at me.

"Oh, thanks." I took the green envelope and flipped it over. There was no return address, but the postmark read Outer Banks, North Carolina.

Gwenny scooted in closer. "Outer Banks? North Carolina?"

I nodded. "Who do we know in North Carolina?" I asked, running my finger under the glue and pulling out a card.

My sister shrugged and leaned in, and I playfully held the card so she couldn't see.

"Oh, stop it." She giggled and tugged the card down so we were both looking at it.

Gwenny was the one person who could make me genuinely smile. Two years younger than me, she was my polar opposite. Free spirited, blond, skinny, full of personality, laid back, easy to get along with, and got great grades without opening a single book. I had every right to be jealous of her, but had never once been. She was just too . . . well, amazing. I wished I could be more like her.

I read the card out loud.

Dear Elizabeth Margaret,
Happy Graduation! I'm so very proud of you.
I'd like to invite you to spend the summer with me at my
B & B, the Pepper House, here in the Outer Banks. Have
your mom or grandmother call me if you're interested.
Love and smiles,
Your Aunt Tilly (Matilda)

Gwenny gave me a little push. "Get out! We have an aunt? Would that be Dad's or Mom's sister?"

"I have no clue." I read the note again, confused. *This couldn't be possible—a chance to get away?*

Mom strolled into the living room, her sensible heels clicking on the hardwood floor announcing her arrival. Running her thumb over her BlackBerry, she scanned her messages as she walked, always working. You'd have to be if you ran the pediatric ward at the nearby hospital.

She glanced up. "Hello, girls. Studying?"

Gwenny plucked the card from my hands and held it up. "Who's Aunt Tilly?"

Mom nearly tripped over her own feet as she stopped dead in her tracks. She brought her gaze straight to Gwenny and just stood there, staring at her, her face a shade paler than normal.

"Matilda?" she whispered.

Gwenny's blond brows lifted as she waved the card in the air. "Em just got a graduation card from an Aunt Tilly."

Mom stared at the card. I couldn't remember ever having seen her so stunned. It made me very curious.

Impatient, Gwenny got up and took the card to Mom.

Mom cleared her throat, more composed now, and slid her BlackBerry into her leather hip holster as she grasped the card. "I've told you about Matilda. You've just forgotten."

Gwenny rolled a look my way, as if to say, yeah, right.

"She's my younger sister, by ten years," Mom mumbled as she opened the card.

I watched her read it, my heart picking up pace, wondering what was going on.

"Grandmother's coming to dinner tonight," Mom said, abruptly changing the subject. "Please be ready by seven o'clock. And don't wear jeans. You know how much your grandmother hates to see you girls in jeans." And with that, she clicked her way back across the hardwood floor, my card still in her hand.

My sister spun around. "What was that?"

"I have no idea, but we're going to find out who this Matilda is."

Gwenny gave an excited hop. "Count me in!"

* * *

About an hour later, I passed by my mom's office on the way upstairs to Gwenny's room. Even though a thick wood door separated me from my mom, her muffled voice filtered through. She was speaking with someone on the phone, and she did not sound happy.

I lingered in the hallway, tempted to smash my ear against the door and see if the phone call was about this mysterious Aunt Tilly.

"Elizabeth Margaret?"

I jumped and turned around. "Dad! Um, hi."

He glanced at the closed door. "Are you being nosy?"

"Uh, no, sir." I hurried past him. "See you at dinner."

As I headed up the stairs to my sister's room, I heard him open and close my mom's door. I wondered if he knew the story behind Matilda or if Mom was keeping him in the dark too. It wouldn't be the first time.

"Hey, it's me," I said, opening Gwenny's door.

"Guess what?" she turned and excitedly whispered, pointing to her laptop on her desk. "I found Matilda."

"What? No way!" I hurried over to look. "Mom's downstairs arguing with someone on the phone. I think it's about Matilda."

Gwenny's eyes widened. "Really? What did you hear?"

"Nothing. Dad busted my attempt at eavesdropping."

"Oh."

Gwenny slid into her desk chair and repositioned the laptop so I could see. "Look. She looks just like Mom."

I peered over my sister's shoulder at the screen. She'd found her way to the website of the private school my mom had attended and dug through several alumni links. Several photos depicted my mom all perfect in her graduation gown as she delivered the valedictory speech.

Other photos had Grandmother standing beside her, smiling, and with them a young girl whom I assumed must be Matilda. With her blond hair, blue eyes, and lanky body, Matilda was a smaller version of my mom. "You definitely got their look," I told my sister.

Gwenny laughed. "And you definitely got Grandmother's."

She was right. With my dark features and average height, I was the spitting image of my grandmother.

"So, what else?" I asked, scooting beside Gwenny on her chair.

"Well"—she perked up—"I've got the Pepper House's site and several links to the Outer Banks." While I watched, she pulled up the B&B's website.

It was like something out of a fairy tale, with ivy and bright red flowers growing up both sides of the doorway. There were pictures of the tropical-themed rooms and a beautiful bay out back. There were no photos of Matilda, but there was an e-mail link.

"I can't believe she invited you to come for the whole summer." Gwenny looked over at me. "I'm so jealous. You should let me go in your place. You know, since you've got the internship at dad's firm and all that."

I narrowed my eyes. "No way. This trip is all mine. I've got to get out of this place."

Gwenny raised her eyebrow and shot me a look. "Look at you, being all defiant. Since when do *you* need to get out of here?"

I laughed. "Please. You're the one person who knows I've been feeling . . . out of sorts. I definitely need this."

She sighed. "I would die for an opportunity like this. Snorkeling, beaches, hiking, a cool B&B, an aunt I've never met. And," Gwenny bopped her brows up and down, "a possible hot summer romance."

I smiled.

"I can't believe you are going to do this!" Gwenny went on. "You're always following the rules. Little Miss Valedictorian, eyes on the prize, going to conquer the world someday. You're way too good. You make me look horrible. But this? It's your last summer of freedom before Mom and Dad really get their claws into you. I'm so proud of you for not passing this up."

"Now I just have to convince Mom and Dad."

A knock sounded on the door, and Gwenny quickly turned the laptop. "Yes?"

Mom peeked her head in. "You girls need to get ready for dinner. Grandmother will be here soon."

We both nodded.

She gave us one of those what-are-you-up-to looks, which we both pretended to innocently ignore. "Forty five minutes," she warned us before closing the door.

Gwenny sighed. "Well, I need to take a shower."

She grabbed her stuff and disappeared into her bathroom as I went back to her laptop. While she showered, I clicked some more through the Pepper House's sparse website. Then I went on to research more on the Outer Banks. The more I surfed, the more I really did want to take my aunt up on her offer. Even if my parents said no, I was going to find a way to get there.

* * *

Forty-seven minutes later (and dressed not in jeans), my sister and I entered the formal living room, where our grandmother sat sipping a martini.

I'd seen her once a week since I could remember, but I never felt comfortable around her.

"Granddaughters," she formally greeted us. "You are late."

"Only by two minutes," Gwenny replied, and I repressed a smile. I'd never challenge my grandmother, but somehow Gwenny always got away with it.

"Sorry," I dutifully apologized, giving her a light kiss on her cheek.

Grandmother surveyed me and then Gwenny. "Elizabeth Margaret, you've put on a few pounds."

I sighed. I knew that was coming. I loved food, and my metabolism was terrible. Grandmother never had a problem pointing that out. Frankly, I wanted to blame it on her. After all, she was the one I took after.

"Grandmother, she looks fine," Gwenny defended me.

I loved my sister, for more reasons than I could count, but her willingness to stand up to Grandmother for me always topped the list.

"Girls," my dad greeted us from his leather chair.

We both turned and smiled.

Our dad was very handsome. Tall, trim, brown hair, wire-framed glasses, and always dressed in slacks and a nice shirt.

My mom stood and smoothed the lines of her linen suit. "Shall we eat?"

A few minutes later we were seated around the freshly polished dining room table. Mom's best china, crystal, and silver decorated each place setting. She used it once a week, when Grandmother came.

Navia, our housekeeper, had made dinner, as she did almost every night, and had it simmering along the buffet. I smiled at her, and she winked back at me as she ducked into the kitchen.

I had actually helped make dinner, but no one except Gwenny knew that. I'd been sneaking into the kitchen to help Navia for as long as I could remember. My mom had caught me once and gotten really mad.

"I don't pay Navia for you to do her work," Mom had angrily spat. "You are not in this world *to cook*. You will be cooked for. Do you hear me, young lady?"

My mom didn't get angry often, but when she did, she meant business. I had been ten at the time and so shocked at her forcefulness, I barely managed a nod. It had taken months and Gwenny's persistence to finally convince me to sneak back in and continue helping Navia.

Cooking made me happy. Only Gwenny knew I held a secret fantasy to be a chef someday. My parents and grandmother would absolutely flip if I ever put a voice to that dream.

We served ourselves from the buffet and began eating. Usually my grandmother had a million questions about school for Gwenny and me, but tonight no one spoke. Gwenny and I kept glancing around and shooting each other questioning looks.

"Elizabeth Margaret," my grandmother finally broke the silence.

I quickly looked at my sister first, then my grandmother. "Yes, ma'am?"

"Your mother tells me you received a graduation card from your aunt Matilda."

My heart skipped a beat. "Yes."

"And she's invited you to spend the summer with her?" Grandmother delicately dabbed her mouth. "Do you have an interest in this?"

"No she does not," my mom answered for me. "She's got the internship at the law firm."

I cut another glance at my sister, and she gave me an encouraging nod in return.

"Actually, yes, I am interested," I quickly countered before I lost my nerve.

My mom just looked at me.

"I'm sorry," I said, experiencing the frustration I frequently felt with my family whenever I said exactly what I wanted to.

"Elizabeth Margaret," my dad interrupted. "Do you know how much trouble I went through to get you this internship?"

"Yes," I answered, wishing I had just kept my mouth shut. "I know, but—"

"Do you know how important this is," Mom railroaded on, "for your future? Harvard is expecting it."

My shoulders dropped.

"Do you know—"

"Yes," I rudely interrupted my dad. "I know. OK?"

"Watch your tone, young lady," Grandmother rebuked me.

I sighed and looked at first my mom, then my dad, then my grandmother. They all held matching disappointed expressions. Under the table, Gwenny touched her foot to mine in an encouraging gesture.

Bringing my gaze back to my mom, I straightened my shoulders. "Look, I've done everything you have ever asked of me. My grades are impeccable, I'm going to an Ivy League university, my future is set. I'm not asking for a lot here. I just want to step away, have some fun, and enjoy my final summer before college. Can't you all understand that? Didn't you ever feel overwhelmed? Like you just need to take a breath? That's how I feel. That's how I've felt for a while now. And it's not like I'm going to be with strangers. This is my aunt. What do you think is going to happen?"

I stopped and took a breath. I couldn't believe I'd just said all that. Out of the corner of my eye, I caught my sister smiling at my outspoken self, and I watched my parents and grandmother exchange an unreadable look.

Grandmother took a sip of her coffee. "What about your responsibilities here? The internship. The prestige of that alone . . ."

I glanced at my dad. I really didn't want to disappoint him. With the way he'd been talking about it, I think he was more excited about this internship than I was.

I kept staring at him, waiting for him to respond, but he didn't say anything.

I took a deep breath and gathered my thoughts. "Dad, I understand what you went through to get the internship slot for me. I know I was picked from over a hundred applicants. I realize that. And I don't want to disappoint you. You know that, right?"

My dad cleared his throat. "Of course."

"But I also don't want to pass up this opportunity that Aunt Matilda has given me. Maybe . . ." I glanced between my parents, an idea forming, "maybe I can spend a month with Matilda and then come back and finish the summer at your firm?"

Actually, that wasn't a bad idea. That way I'd get what I want, still uphold the promise I made to my dad, and not disappoint my family—or Harvard.

I looked across the table at my grandmother to see her nod approvingly.

My parents exchanged another look and my dad gave a small nod.

"Fine," Mom spoke. "One month there and then you'll definitely come back here for the internship."

I nodded, squashing the urge to squeal with delight. "Definitely."

My mom took a sip of her wine. "I'll call Matilda and arrange everything."

Chapter Two

"Oh my God, I can't *believe* you're going. I am *so* jealous," Gwenny said later that night, closing my door and hopping on my bed.

I sat up. "I know. I can't believe I'm going either. And I can't believe I actually said all that at dinner . . . in front of Grandmother."

"Well, it was awesome! What are you going to do with one whole month in paradise?"

"I don't know. I was just lying here thinking about it. You know, I'd love to go sailing."

Gwenny waved me off. "Oh please. You sound like Mom. You've been sailing. Loosen up. Try something else." She thought a second. "Ooh!" Gwenny grabbed my foot. "It's a B&B, right?"

"Right."

"You should ask Aunt Matilda if you can help out in the kitchen. Take your recipe book with you. I bet you can teach her chef a thing or two."

I immediately shook my head. "No way. What if it got back to Mom?"

Gwenny got off my bed and went over to my desk where I had my cookbooks hidden. Mom would have a cow if she saw my stash of culinary books, let alone knew I wanted to cook.

"Seriously, this is a perfect opportunity," Gwenny said, flipping through one of my books. "You love to cook. You have loads of fab recipes here."

I took the book and leafed through the pages.

She was right—I should take this moment and use it to do something I loved. "Maybe you're right."

She jumped off my bed. "Of course I am. Oh, and we've totally got to go shopping for you. You need a bikini."

I laughed. "I have a bikini."

Gwenny crinkled her nose. "Really? That blue-and-white one?"

I threw a pillow at her. "There's nothing wrong with that bikini."

She sighed. "You obviously aren't too concerned about a hot summer romance. That bikini's better suited for running a triathlon or something. Talk about unappealing."

"Gwenny!"

"What? You need strings." She bounced her brows. "And cleavage."

I just shook my head, imagining myself in a tiny bikini. "I wouldn't be able to do anything but lie around. I'd spill right out of it."

"And that's bad why?"

I rolled my eyes.

"Whatever. And when we look for a new bikini, we can pick up a dress for Ryan's end-of-the-year party. You're going, right?"

"Ugh." I made a face. "Do I have to?"

"Yes. Because Mom and Dad won't let me go unless you're there."

"Why do you want to go so badly? You don't even like half the people who will be there. Neither do I."

"Um, duh. Logan will be there?"

"Oh, yeah, Logan," I teased. "Your irresistible crush. All right, I'll go. It's the least I can do for my little sister."

She gave me a quick hug and bounded out of my room.

I smiled. I was seriously going to miss her.

* * *

The next morning I sat in our living room going over my notes for the physics final I would take in a few hours. I'd been reading and rereading the same paragraphs and getting absolutely nothing done. I was way too distracted now with Aunt Matilda's offer and the exciting possibilities it brought to actually focus on the two finals I had left to take and the three short days until I departed for what I hoped would be the summer of my life.

Why had my mom and grandmother never mentioned my

aunt? Was there something about Matilda they didn't want Gwenny or me to know?

"Elizabeth Margaret?"

I glanced up and saw my mom sitting at the grand piano across the living room. Behind her a bank of spotless windows stretched the length of our living room, and beyond that the Cambridge side of the Charles River.

Mom played every morning. She said it calmed her before a hectic day at the hospital.

With a delicate sigh, she rolled the piano bench out and stood. As if on cue a ray of sunlight shot through the cloudy May sky, illuminating the area around her.

As I had many times before, I wondered if I would ever develop my mom's grace and style. She was perfect, envied by everyone—slim, beautiful, controlled.

But then none of the people who envied her had to actually live with her perfection.

"Elizabeth Margaret?"

I gave my head a little shake. "Sorry, yes?"

She looked at me, slowly arching her left brow. I knew that arch. It meant she was about to say something that I should take very seriously. "I want you to remember you're a lady. You're an *educated* young woman. Matilda does things . . . her own way. She's dramatic, emotional, unreasonable. When you're there, with her, just remember where you come from and how good you have it."

"Mom, I'll be fine," I reassured her. "I'm going to go, enjoy my month, and come back refreshed and ready for my internship and my freshman year at Harvard. I'm not going to forget who I am and become someone else just by visiting Aunt Matilda."

A soft smile slowly crept onto my mom's face. She closed the leather binder that held her sheet music and crossed the hardwood floor to where I sat. Leaning down, she kissed the top of my head. "You're something else, you know that, Elizabeth Margaret? You make your dad and me very proud."

I smiled. It wasn't often she gave praise.

I watched her stroll from the living room, glad I'd said everything I had. Even though I said it only because I knew she wanted to hear it.

I wanted this to be the best month ever—one that I would never forget.

* * *

Two days later I'd aced all my finals and stood outside of school saying good-bye to my friends. With most of us going to different universities, I wondered if we'd really stay in touch after graduation.

"Did I tell you I'm going to Greece for the summer?" Fiona asked, as if she hadn't asked that question a million times before.

I smiled a little. "Yes, Fiona, you did mention it."

"Of course, my dad doesn't realize," she smiled secretly, "Ryan will be there too."

"Of course," I agreed, glancing around for Gwenny.

Lilia grabbed my arm. "I got into Yale. Did Mother tell your mom?"

"Actually you told me," I reminded her. Months ago, I added silently.

"Oh." She giggled. "That's right."

We all knew she got into Yale because her grandfather had made a huge donation. But Lilia wanted to think it was on her credentials alone.

"Hey!" Gwenny bounded up beside me.

"Hey," I said, giving Gwenny a thank-God-you're-here smile.

Ryan sidled up behind Fiona and grabbed her around the waist. He pulled her back and whispered something into her ear that elicited a sexy little chuckle from Fiona.

I watched them flirt, wishing for a short moment that I'd had a boyfriend—or even one date—in high school. But being valedictorian was more important, so I'd focused on that. I'd have plenty of time for romance later—at least, that's what I had told myself. Now I wasn't so sure.

"I hear you're going to visit a crazy aunt for the summer?" Ryan asked.

"Crazy?" I looked at Gwenny. "Who said she was crazy?"

Gwenny shrugged. "Not me."

"All distant unknown secret relatives are crazy," Lilia said. "It's practically a fact."

"Well, mine isn't," I said defensively.

"Whatever." Lilia checked her cell phone for messages.

"You coming to the end-of-the-year party tonight?" Fiona asked. "Ryan's dad opened his Boston condo for us. There'll be plenty of alcohol," she enticed in a singsongy voice.

I smiled, thinking of Gwenny's crush. "Yeah, we'll be there for a little while. Not too long, though. I have to pack."

Fiona pouted a little. "All right. Well, we'll party hard while you're there."

"Sure," I agreed, even though Fiona knew I wasn't a partier.

She gave me a quick hug, then grabbed Ryan's hand and headed toward the parking lot.

Ryan looked back with a wave.

"See ya," Lilia said, still looking at her phone, turning toward the parking lot as well. "Call me if you want a lift later."

Gwenny and I headed toward the parking lot too. We were going to the mall before heading home. I needed a pink shirt to go with a white skirt I had. And I knew exactly which shirt I wanted.

* * *

"Oh!" Gwenny pointed to a bathing-suit shop near the mall's entrance. "Let's go in there!"

"My suit is fine," I assured her, then cut off toward Nordstrom.

"Um . . ." She held back. "I'm going to grab some toasted pecans. Want some?"

"Sure. Meet me by Cosmetics in ten." I knew exactly where my top was, so I snagged it off the rack, paid, and met Gwenny. Then we wandered the mall for a little while, sharing pecans and shopping for a dress for her, but we found nothing.

When we got home, I headed straight to my room and began packing.

Taking a white cotton T-shirt from my dresser, I slid it

beneath my plaid capris and put a dark brown scarf in between them. I took a step back and surveyed the piles of neatly folded clothes.

From my bedside table, I took my legal pad with its comprehensive list and began checking off items, smiling at my thoroughness.

My sister came through my open door and surveyed the clothes stacked neatly on my bed. "Seriously? You're way too organized for your own good."

I smiled. "I'll take that as a compliment."

She handed me a gift bag. "A going-away present."

"Gwenny! You didn't have to do anything," I said, putting down my checklist.

"Oh, shush, and open."

I lifted the gift paper away and looked inside. "What is this?"

Gwenny grinned.

I reached in and pulled out a black bikini with gold trim. Holding it up by its thin strap, I merely looked at my sister. "Let me guess. The bathing-suit shop in the mall?"

"What? That blue-and-white one is so not going to work."

Playfully, I rolled my eyes and tossed it into my suitcase. "Fine. Thank you."

My dad peeked his head in. "When are you ladies leaving for your party?"

"Not for another couple of hours," I answered.

"No drinking," he warned. "And be home by midnight."

My sister and I nodded.

He headed off and my sister sat down on the edge of the

bed. She didn't say anything for a while, just sat there watching me pack.

"Everything OK?" I asked softly.

Gwenny sighed. "I'm really going to miss you, Em."

I stopped packing and smiled. It wasn't often my lighthearted sister got serious.

"I'm going to miss you, too."

She raised her sad blue eyes to mine. "It's going to be so boring here without you. And I'm going to have to deal with Grandmother on my own! You need to e-mail, text, call, send smoke signals—whatever—and tell me everything you're doing."

I laughed. "Yes, I know. Every day. I promise."

Gwenny got up and shuffled over to my desk. She got my favorite cookbook and slowly slipped it into my suitcase. "And don't forget this."

I smiled.

"Now"—she bounced her brows—"for the party tonight, I was thinking of wearing my denim miniskirt and silver tank. Logan-worthy?"

I nodded. "Definitely Logan-worthy!"

Chapter Three

The party came and went and my sister and Logan totally hit it off. He couldn't stop looking at her, actually. For a split second, I was envious—I hoped someday someone would look at me that way.

After saying good-bye to everyone, we headed home, and despite the late hour, I decided to finish packing. It was fine, though. There was no way I would be able to sleep.

By the time morning came, I was dressed and ready to go before anyone else was even awake.

Several agonizingly slow hours later, Dad loaded the car, and after a long, sappy good-bye to Gwenny (and a proper, short good-bye with Mom), he dropped me at the airport.

My plane flew into Raleigh, North Carolina, and after a frustratingly long delay I took a puddle jumper to the island.

My aunt lived on the farthest island out in the Atlantic Ocean. It wasn't actually connected to the Outer Banks but was still considered part of it.

Looping my leather carry-on over my shoulder, I disembarked the plane into a sunny June afternoon. I made my way into the small airport and to the baggage claim and stood at the carousel watching luggage go around and around for what seemed like an eternity. My black hard case never cycled into view.

I sighed. I'd hoped everything would go smoothly. Hiking my carry-on up my shoulder, I headed into the small office, where I stepped up to the counter.

"Here, fill this out," a woman said before I could utter a word.

"Uh, oh, OK." I took the form and filled out all the pertinent information: size, color, name brand, and contents.

"We'll most likely deliver it by midnight tonight," the baggage lady told me as I handed her the form.

I sighed again, knowing the drill. I'd lost luggage before. "I'm not seeing my suitcase anytime soon, am I?"

She shot me a fake smile. "We'll call you as soon as it comes in."

"Thanks," I mumbled, sliding my paperwork off the counter.

My mom had told me my aunt would be picking me up, but when I walked from baggage claim to the outside, the gravel parking area was nearly empty. There were only three vehicles in the entire lot. I squinted against the sun and into the cars, but didn't see anyone waiting for me.

I dug my cell phone from my purse and dialed the number to the B&B.

Five, six, seven rings. Just as I was about to click off, someone answered. *"Yello?"*

"Is this the Pepper House?"

"The one and only," the man confirmed.

"This is Elizabeth Margaret call—"

"Oh, Elizabeth Margaret! We're all so excited to meet you!"

I smiled a little and breathed a sigh of relief at a friendly voice.

"I'm Domino, the Pepper House's cook. Did Cade make it to you OK?"

"I'm sorry, who?"

"Cade. He works here. Your aunt had a last-minute thing with one of the guests. Something about an allergy to hibiscus. Of course, we don't grow hibiscus here, but she—the guest, that is—is convinced the red flowers in her cottage are hibiscus. We even showed her pictures of hibiscus and she doesn't believe us. Or she believes us, but she thinks the red flowers might be a distant strand of the hi—"

"Excuse me, Domino?"

"—biscus. Yeah?"

"You were saying something about my ride," I reminded him.

"Oh, yeah. Cade. He should've been there by now."

"Really? I don't see him. May I have his cell number so I can call him?"

"Cell phone?" Domino let out a booming laugh. "Oh, sweetie. This is going to be some summer for you. Cade doesn't have one of those." He laughed again. "He'll get there when he gets there. No worries. He probably stopped off somewhere. It's island time around here."

My entire life currently did and always had operated around strict schedules. So I wasn't sure I knew how to do "island time." "Um, isn't there someone else who can come for me? Or should I take a cab?"

"Well, the only cabdriver stopped service about an hour ago. He's real scheduled with his evening fishing."

"Evening fishing?"

"Yeah. And as far as someone else coming to get you, I'm sorry, but no can do."

"Oh. Well . . ."

"We've got one van, and Cade took off in it a while ago." He paused, then said, "Are you sure he's not there yet?"

"What?" I looked around. "Um, no."

"Well, we're on one end of the island and the airport's on the other. Ten miles between us. Speed limit's forty-five. Like I said Cade must've stopped. Plus, it's the end of the day, so there might be traffic. If old man Hester is herding his goats . . ."

I looked around as Domino continued giving me all the scenarios. "That's OK," I finally interrupted. "I'll find a place to sit and wait."

"Sounds great, sweetie! See you soon!"

"OK, then." I clicked off.

A couple of minutes passed, and I stood there staring at the parking lot, waiting for the van to appear.

Finally I crossed back to the airport's exit door, planning to wait in the air-conditioned interior. I gave it a push and found it locked.

With a sigh, I scooted over to a low concrete wall and sat down.

My cell buzzed, jolting me a bit. I pulled it out, saw it was my mom, and hit the Talk button. "Hello, Mom. I'm here."

"Any problems?"

Not wanting to recount everything so far, I replied cheerfully, "Nope. Everything's fine. Just waiting on my ride from the airport."

"So . . . you haven't seen Matilda yet?"

"No, not yet."

"Well, I'm sure she'll be there soon. OK, then. We'll talk in a few days."

"Say hi to Gwenny for me."

"I will. Take care." And with that, she clicked off.

With one last glance around for Cade and the van, I put the phone back in my bag, pulled on my floppy hat and sunglasses, dug out my *Culinary Schools of the World* book from my carry-on, and started leafing through it.

My mind drifted to my upcoming freshman year of college and the pre-law classes I would be taking. I was going to be a lawyer. That had always been the plan. I'd tried many times to picture myself in a courtroom arguing a case, but somehow I just couldn't see it. Confrontation was not my strong point. Neither was debate. Maybe I'd be better suited for nonlitigation—something that would keep me at a desk all day. As I imagined my first real job, I felt my mind drifting and let my eyes close . . .

You Elizabeth Margaret?

In my dreamless sleep I mumbled a response.

Hello?

I wedged one of my eyes open.

Along the curb sat an old green van with the sun setting behind it. A blond-haired guy wearing red board shorts and a white tank top leaned against the driver's door. Silver shades hid his eyes, and his wavy hair fell almost to his shoulders. His tan said he lived in the sun. The words "sexy loser"—one of Gwenny's favorite sayings—popped into my mind.

He hitched his chin. "You Elizabeth Margaret?"

"Yes. Let me guess." I got to my feet. "Cade."

He gave one affirmative nod. "That'd be me."

I glanced at my watch, blinked, and refocused. "Do you realize you're two hours late?"

Cade sighed. "Yeah."

I stood there a second. *Yeah?* That's all this guy had to say?

He opened the door and got in.

I grabbed my stuff scattered around my feet and hurried across the concrete to the van.

Behind his sunglasses, I saw Cade glance up questioningly at my floppy hat.

I slipped it off my head. "Did you get a flat tire or something?"

"Or something," he said with a nod, and cranked the engine. "You getting in, or what?"

It took me a second to realize this guy wasn't going to apologize for being late, or even offer an explanation.

He looked beyond me. "Where's your suitcase?"

I headed around the hood of the van, opened the passenger door, and climbed in. "Seems it didn't make the connection."

"Oh." He ground the van into gear and pulled out of the parking lot.

As he drove, I looked over at Cade. I knew guys like him. The guys at school—too good-looking. Knew he was good-looking. Arrogant. Cocky. All the girls fell all over him. Thought he was God's gift to the world.

Cade shifted gears, flipped the radio to a reggae station, and turned the volume low.

With a deep breath, I decided I was not going to let any of this irritate me. I was here for one whole month, and I was going to enjoy every moment. I propped my arm in the open window, inhaled the warm, salty air, and took in the early evening scenery.

Off to the right stretched the blue expanse of the Atlantic Ocean. The miles of sparkling clarity reminded me of the waters of Bermuda. My family had gone there two years ago for summer vacation. Gwenny and I had swum and snorkeled until our skin turned wrinkly.

On the horizon I caught sight of a fishing boat with lines and nets thrown out.

A moped passed us, beeping its tiny horn. I wondered how fast we were going. Cade glanced over and gave a slight nod to the older man as he went zipping past.

We continued along the coastal highway with the ocean to my right and overgrown brush to the left. We passed a small village of stone cottages nearly hidden by the overgrown greenery, and I inched forward in my seat to catch a better glimpse.

Eventually, the van reached the other side of the island and pulled off the highway onto a gravel road.

We drove under the beautiful archway of bright red flowers growing on thick green vines that I had seen on the Pepper House's website. We circled around a stone fountain with four carved goats spouting water from their mouths. Cade stopped the van in front of a Mediterranean-style whitewashed stone house covered in more beautiful red flowers.

He turned the key and silence filled the cab.

"Here we are," he said, flinging open his door and getting out of the van.

I sat for a moment and smiled. *Here I am.*

Chapter Four

"Elizabeth Margaret!" The door to the Pepper House flew open and out shot a whirl of color. "Welcome!"

Laughing, a tall woman opened the van door and pulled me out and straight into a huge hug. After a few seconds, she gripped my shoulders and with a huge grin held me at arm's length. "*You* are gorgeous!"

I blinked. "Um, thank you." And smiled a little. "You must be Aunt Matilda."

"Matilda? My gosh, no one's called me that since I was a kid. It's Tilly."

With another laugh, she pulled me right back into the tight embrace. So much for the formal greeting I was so used to in my parents' home. Actually, come to think of it, I couldn't think of the last time I had been hugged so tightly.

With her tall, willowy body and blond hair, Tilly was an identical version of my mom. The free-spirited, flowy, younger version of my mom.

She wore colorful pastel bolts of long gauzy fabric that floated and followed her every move, and her hair was loosely pulled back. She thought I was gorgeous? *She* was the gorgeous one. Gorgeous in a natural way.

Aunt Tilly looked straight at Cade. "*Where* have you been?"

"I'll tell you later," he said cryptically, and headed inside.

She watched him walk away, a look of confusion on her face, and then a couple seconds later turned back to me. "I am *so* sorry he made you wait. I would've come and gotten you myself if it weren't for some pesky guests I was dealing with. And we only have one van . . ."

I smiled a little. "That's OK. I'm here now, and that's all that matters."

"Oh"—my aunt hugged me again—"you're so sweet."

She fluttered her fingers at the van. "Let's get your suitcase and get you inside."

I shook my head. "I don't have a suitcase—at least not right now. The airline lost it. I'm hoping it'll be here tomorrow."

"Oh," She fluttered her fingers again. "No worries. You can borrow my clothes until then."

I didn't bother pointing out I was significantly shorter and a bit rounder than her. I doubted anything in her closet would fit.

She grabbed my hand and led me inside. "Are you hungry? Domino is making this fabulous fish dish for dinner."

"Yes, I'm starving. I haven't eaten since the plane from Boston." I glanced at my watch. It was way past my usual dinnertime.

Aunt Tilly closed the door behind us, and I found myself standing in the most interesting room I'd ever seen.

The same whitewashed stone from the exterior made up the interior walls of the spacious living room. Dark wood beams supported the ceiling, where four large wicker-bladed fans hung. They spun slowly, circulating the breeze coming through the open windows.

Along the walls hung vivid paintings of the island. Potted exotic plants decorated every corner. Couches and love seats made out of driftwood were scattered about with flowery cushions and more of those exotic plants between them.

There was no television, only an old-fashioned record player sat in the wood entertainment center. A bookshelf spanned the entire back wall, jam-packed with well-worn hardcovers and paperbacks.

In one corner sat a small table and chairs with a chessboard, pieces out and ready to be played. I *loved* chess. I wondered if Tilly played.

I looked over at her. "I love the décor here. It's very unique and pretty. Almost tropical."

She grinned. "That's exactly what I was going for." She fluttered her fingers through the air. "This is where my guests hang out when they're not out and about." She nodded across to a stone archway on the other side. "Let me show you around a bit."

We crossed the cozy living room, now almost dark from the setting sun. With all the windows, though, I bet this place was bright in the daytime. Aunt Tilly bent to turn on a lamp and we headed through the archway into a dining room.

It looked like the living room with the stone walls and wood-beam rafters. To the left was another archway, leading outside. To the right was a swinging door that I assumed led to the kitchen. Windows lined the entire back wall and looked out over a bay. Six four-seater round tables made of gleaming dark wood scattered the dining room. And more of those wonderful, vibrant paintings decorated the walls.

Aunt Tilly led me over to the bank of windows. Across the small body of water, exterior lights were starting to come on, illuminating cottages, houses, and other buildings.

Aunt Tilly pointed through the window across the bay. "Those are some of the oldest houses on the island. Aren't they beautiful?"

"Very," I agreed.

She tapped on the window. "See that hammock between those two palm trees?"

I nodded.

"Best snoozin' around."

We both smiled at that.

"Come on." She led me from the dining room and out a side door that sat propped open. Lit by ground lights, a pebbled walkway wound away from the main house and disappeared into the trees. "Down that path is one of my cottages." Then she pointed to the right. "And down that path is another. We'll see them tomorrow in the daylight."

"How many guests can you accommodate?"

"The two cottages out there sleep six people each, and tho main house has four bedrooms and baths. Only in season is it full, though. The main house is normally just me and Frederick."

"Frederick?"

Aunt Tilly's blue eyes twinkled. "Your cousin."

I lifted my brows. "I have a cousin?"

She laughed. "Yes, you do. He's fifteen. And"—she tapped me on the nose—"I hope you two find you have things in common. He's a bit serious, though. Maybe you can work on lightening him up while you're here."

This was unbelievable. This place. Tilly. A B&B on an island. A cousin named Frederick. I wondered why my mom and grandmother had kept Aunt Tilly and my cousin a secret.

"Come on, let's get you something to eat." Aunt Tilly linked her fingers in mine and led me back inside, across the dining room, and through a swinging door.

"Boy"—a skinny, bald man pointed a wooden spoon at Cade—"forget about it. You don't need him. You got us. When did you find out he was here, anyway?"

Cade lowered himself onto a barstool. "Just a few hours ago," he moodily answered. "Right before I picked up Elizabeth Margaret."

Aunt Tilly cleared her throat, effectively bringing their attention to us.

I looked at Cade, wondering if the *him* had anything to do with how late Cade had been picking me up.

The skinny man slid a plate of fish and rice in front of Cade, then turned a wide smile to me. "Hello, Elizabeth Margaret. I'm Domino!"

He trotted around the kitchen's center island and stuck out his hand. "It's *so* nice to meet you."

"Hi." I took his hand, falling forward a little as he pumped it up and down.

He stood just a little taller than me, I'd guess maybe five foot six, and looked to be in his sixties.

Domino waved his wooden spoon through the air. "Welcome to my kitchen. This is my domain. Domino's domain." He laughed at his own silly joke. "And you, sweetie, are more than welcome here anytime you want."

I nodded. "Thanks, Domino."

I couldn't help but think about Navia back home and all the times I'd snuck into her kitchen to help. I didn't think I'd be doing much sneaking around here, though. It seemed like everyone was welcome, and I didn't imagine Tilly to be the type to mind my helping out.

The kitchen was exactly what I had expected: one big gas stove with ten burners and side-by-side ovens below; a stainless-steel refrigerator that nearly touched the ceiling; an oversized sink, large enough to wash a kid in; copper pots and pans hanging from a rack over the center island. Six barstools sat around that island, with cupboards along the walls. There was enough room for probably ten people to move about comfortably.

I inhaled deeply. "Something smells wonderful. I heard you cooked fish?"

Domino waved his spoon in the air. "Did I ever!"

Cade slid off his barstool and carried his plate of half-eaten food to the sink. "Catch you guys later."

But he'd only just started eating.

He headed through an archway that led out the back of the kitchen. Halfway through it, he turned back. "Oh, and Elizabeth Margaret?"

I lifted my gaze to his. "Yeah?"

"I'm sorry about picking you up late." His mouth cocked up into a cute little half-smile.

I smiled back. "That's OK."

You don't need him. You got us. When did you find out he was here, anyway?

I played Domino's words back as I watched Cade leave, wondering what was going on, wondering who they had been talking about.

Domino put a plate of food on the counter in front of me. "You eat all that up and I've got Key lime pie for dessert."

I slid onto the barstool. "Aren't you eating?"

"We already did. But I'd love to sit here with you." Aunt Tilly pulled a bottle of white wine from the refrigerator and poured herself a glass.

I took a bite of my fish and my taste buds nearly exploded. "Oh my gosh, this is incredible!" I laughed a little. My mother would have been mortified at my outburst. But . . . this fish was too good not to have an outburst.

Domino smiled. "Thanks."

"I mean it. I've eaten at *the* best restaurants, and this fish is, hands down, the best I've ever had. What *is* this, and how did you make it?"

"Ah." Domino rinsed a dish and put it aside to dry. "It's snapper, and a chef never tells his secrets."

I took another bite, savoring it on my tongue. "Sea salt, ginger, lemon, green onions, tomato, lime, and"—I nibbled another small bite—"soy."

Domino glanced around in surprise. He wagged a soapy finger at me. "That's some palate you have there, sweetie."

Aunt Tilly took a sip of her wine. "Have you ever thought about being a chef?"

For a second I just stared at her. She'd known me exactly two hours and already knew my passion.

I gave a little shrug. "I'm going to be a lawyer and work at my dad's firm."

"Really?" she mumbled as she took another sip. "You don't look like the lawyer type." She paused and smiled. "And you didn't answer my question."

I looked down at my fish. "So," I said, changing the subject, "how long have you owned the Pepper House?"

"Going on ten years now."

I took another bite. "Do you have a big staff?"

"We have a domestic engineer," Domino answered, and Aunt Tilly laughed. "Her name is Beth and she's something else."

"Domestic engineer, as in maid?" I guessed, and they both nodded.

"Call her anything else," Domino added, "and she'll give

you the evil eye. Love brought her here." He glanced at Aunt Tilly. "Love gone wrong, that is."

Tilly rolled her eyes. "Please, Beth bounces back quicker than anybody I know. She's twenty-one now and happier than she's ever been."

I smiled and finished the last few bites of my rice and fish.

"And of course there's Cade," Aunt Tilly continued with the conversation.

"What does he do?"

"You name it, he does it. Landscaping, repairs, transportation . . ."

"So," I joked, "making me wait for two hours isn't normally like him?"

She gave me an affectionate smile. "No, not at all."

I stared at my aunt for a few seconds, feeling an unexpected warmth and affection forming. "You remind me a lot of my sister. Your personality, your looks . . ."

Aunt Tilly winked at me. "I hope to meet Gwyneth someday."

For some reason I found it odd she knew my sister's name when I'd only just recently found out Aunt Tilly even existed. It hit me again how bizarre it was that I had another whole family right here that I hardly knew anything about. "I call her Gwenny."

"Gwenny. That's cute."

I suddenly wanted to ask Tilly all about my mom and grandmother and what happened between them and why she was kept a secret all these years. But I didn't want to be rude.

That would be a conversation for another day, hopefully.

"*Mom?*" echoed a guy's voice through the bed and breakfast.

"Kitchen!" Aunt Tilly yelled back before looking at me. "That's Frederick. He's been at the library."

Very curious and definitely excited to meet my cousin, I slid back onto my barstool. It was a good thing I was sitting down because when he walked in, it was like looking in a mirror.

He had the same dark curly hair, brown eyes, and olive skin that I did. He could be my brother.

"Hey," my cousin greeted me. "Glad to see somebody else got our grandmother's genes."

I chuckled. "I was just thinking that."

With a warm smile, Frederick held his hand out in a much more formal greeting than his exuberant mom. He was neatly groomed and preppy. Only his flip-flops hinted at a beachy feel. Looking into his dark eyes, I gave his hand a shake, and had an immediate, distinct feeling we were going to be good friends. I couldn't wait to tell Gwenny about him.

I glanced down to the book he held. "Ooh, what are you reading?"

"Something from my summer list. *Frankenstein.*"

I scrunched my lips. "Not my favorite. My sister, Gwenny, is reading that this summer too. You guys are the same age, right?"

Frederick glanced at his mom for confirmation. "I think."

Aunt Tilly nodded. "That's right. You're both going to be juniors. You're older by two months."

Frederick put his book down and, playfully poking Domino

in the ribs, crossed to the fridge and got out the pie. "Chess club's been canceled this week."

Aunt Tilly nodded. "I'm not surprised, with summer break and all."

"Yes," Frederick agreed, then turned to me. "Do you play?"

"I do, and I'd be up for a game anytime. I was president of my school chess club," I said, being playfully obnoxious.

Frederick clicked the refrigerator door closed and laughed. "I accept your challenge. In fact, I'm glad you're here. No one else around here knows a pawn from a knight."

"Oh, jeez," Domino said, "now we've got two brainiacs to deal with this summer."

Frederick and I exchanged a small smile and I watched as he rifled around for a fork and plate. He was short for a guy and very adorable in his wire-framed glasses.

"Have you seen your room?" Frederick asked me.

"Not yet."

Aunt Tilly took another sip of her wine. "Why don't you give her the rest of the tour when you get done?"

Frederick took a bite of pie and wiped his mouth. "Sounds good."

My phone rang, and I dug it out of my bag. It was past nine at night. Maybe it was Gwenny. "Grandmother," I said instead, looking at the caller ID.

No one said a word, and I got the distinct impression my grandmother wasn't exactly the most loved person around here.

"Hello?" I answered, eyeing my aunt.

Tilly suddenly became very interested in the depths of her wineglass. I glanced over and saw Frederick studying his pie like it was a piece of art. And Domino was putting a little *too* much effort into wiping the counter.

"Elizabeth Margaret, did you make it to your aunt's?" my grandmother asked.

"Yes. I'm sitting here in the kitchen visiting with everyone."

"I tried calling Matilda earlier on her house phone, but she didn't answer. Put her on," Grandmother requested, not even bothering to exchange pleasantries with me.

I handed my cell to my aunt. "Um, she wants to talk to you."

Aunt Tilly took her time reaching over and taking the phone from me. She put it to her ear. "Mother?"

My grandmother's muffled voice bled through the phone. It wasn't an angry voice, but it wasn't exactly nice, either. More stern. Matter-of-fact. And it made my aunt visibly tense.

I kept my gaze glued to Aunt Tilly and tried my best to eavesdrop.

Aunt Tilly sighed and began rubbing her temples.

My grandmother could do a number on someone.

A few minutes later, Aunt Tilly mumbled something and then she hit End.

Her face looked utterly exhausted, but she pasted the biggest, fakest smile on as she handed the cell back to me.

"It's nice to know I'm not the only one Grandmother yells at," I made a feeble attempt at a joke.

Aunt Tilly didn't respond and instead said, "Frederick, why don't you show your cousin to her room?" And with that, Aunt Tilly got off her stool and left the kitchen.

Chapter Five

Stifling a yawn, I followed Frederick up a flight of stone steps. He led the way down a wide hallway. Two doors sat open off the left side of the corridor.

"That one's Mom's," Frederick indicated, pointing into a room with the most beautiful canopy bed I'd ever seen. Filmy fabric was draped over the structure and flowing with the breeze from the open windows. The room definitely seemed to suit what I knew of my aunt.

"And this one's mine," he indicated, nodding into a room that looked like something straight out of a history book, complete with a globe, telescope, books, and no electronics.

And then it occurred to me. "I haven't seen a television anywhere."

He nodded. "That's right."

"Is that on purpose?"

"Absolutely. Our guests don't come here to watch TV. They come here to relax. If they want technology, they can go to one of the resorts or the local bar for sports."

"And you're OK with that?" No one I knew of would be OK with that.

He pointed to a laptop I hadn't seen on his bed. "That's my connection to the outside world. We do have Wi-Fi here."

I laughed. "I'll be borrowing that."

"No prob." He nodded to the two rooms across the hall. "And there are two empty bedrooms—you can take whichever one you'd like. Each has its own bathroom."

I smiled. "Thanks."

"Sure." Frederick stepped into his room. "Well, yell if you need anything. I'll be in here digging through the first chapter of . . ." He held the summer reading book up.

"OK. Let me know if you want to discuss the finer points of reanimation."

He smiled at that, and as he closed his door halfway, I wandered across to the two available bedrooms, picked the one closest to Frederick's, dropped my meager belongings on the floor, and flopped across the bed.

I got out my cell and texted Gwenny. U WOULD LUV IT HERE.

A few seconds later, my phone beeped with a response. SHUT UP! I'M SO JEALOUS.

AUNT IS GREAT. SHE REMINDS ME OF U.

REALLY?!

U 2 LOOK EXACTLY ALIKE.

SHE'S GORGEOUS 2 HUH?

I laughed at my silly sister's pretend conceit. AND SHE SEEMS FUN.

OH, EM, I WISH I WAS THERE.

ME TOO. I yawned. SLEEPY. WE'LL TALK 2MORO.

I stared up at the wooden beams lining my ceiling and thought over everything that had happened in this very long day. And as my thoughts drifted, my eyes closed. . . .

* * *

The next morning I awoke to the sound of singing—loud, very off-key, singing. I smiled, quickly remembering where I was.

I noticed then that someone had laid a blanket over me, and I sat up. My bedroom looked different in the morning light. Sunny. Warm. Friendly. And with the large fan circling over top of me, very welcoming.

As I stretched I looked around and noticed a painting on the wall. Looking at the swirl of color, at the real-life depiction of a family in a sailboat, I smiled. I wanted to climb right into that picture and dive into the clear water. I'd have to remember and ask my aunt about the artist.

More off-key singing brought me to focus again, and I peered out the window to see dark green leaves and red flowers. A small bit of wind trickled in and I inhaled the sweet scent.

I swung off the bed and padded across the room to my bathroom. With its pedestal sink and claw-foot tub, it rounded out the unique charm of the house.

I brushed my teeth and found my way downstairs to the kitchen.

"Morning," I said as I walked in.

Domino stood by the stove flipping pancakes and singing. "Hey!" he said, looking up. "We were wondering when you'd finally come back to the living."

I chuckled. "Smells good." I sniffed again. "What else are you making besides pancakes?"

Narrowing his eyes, Domino waved his spatula at me. "Not telling. I'm going to feed you and see if that talented palate of yours can decipher it."

I smiled. "I'm up for the challenge."

Aunt Tilly swung through the doors carrying a tray of dirty dishes. "Cottage One's checking out today." She caught sight of me and her eyes lit up. "Hi, gorgeous!"

My smile got a little wider.

Aunt Tilly looked awesome. Glowing. Her hair hung in long blond layers down her back. She wore another flowy, lightweight outfit, and thin bracelets clinked on both wrists.

She put her tray down on the center island. "You need some fresh clothes. Go sift through my closet and see what works."

"Aunt Tilly." I paused, trying not to hurt her feelings and at the same time a little embarrassed. "In case you haven't noticed"—I pointed to my body—"I'm not exactly your size."

She tsked me. "Nonsense. Go on up. If you don't find anything, well, then it'll give us an excuse to go shopping."

I shrugged and turned to Domino. "Save that palate challenge. I'll be back in a few." Tilly shooed me off and I trudged up the stairs, not exactly looking forward to what I was sure was a futile exercise. I entered my aunt's bedroom and headed to her closet. A multitude of colorful, lightweight, flowy garments hung in jammed, jumbled rows.

I sifted through them, checking the sizes. A peach-colored sundress caught my attention and I pulled it off the packed rack. It sprang free, along with several other dresses and a couple of hats. A bundle of scarves snagged on a shelf above, sending some books sliding down.

I picked everything up and sort of stuck it back in where I could. As I put the last book back, I caught sight of one that had family pics printed on the spine.

I pulled it down again and opened the cover. On page one was a candid shot of Aunt Tilly and Domino having a water fight outside the Pepper House. I smiled, almost hearing their laughter.

The next page showed my aunt with what looked like a young Cade building a sandcastle.

Frederick and my aunt came next, doubling on a moped.

Then my aunt, a dark-haired man, and Frederick posing in the living room. I wondered if the man was Frederick's father.

Several more pages showed my cousin and Cade goofing off. Clearly, he was a big part of this family.

I flipped the thick album paper a few more pages to find a formal shot of my grandmother, mother, and Aunt Tilly when she was probably a little younger than me. None of them smiled. I shook my head, not at all surprised.

Then there came a row of pictures of me, starting when I was just a baby and going until now. I spotted a few of Gwenny, too.

"Hey," Aunt Tilly said, and I jumped. She glanced at the

album and cleared her voice. "Oh, well, look what you found." She tried to sound cheerful, but something in her voice made her sound guarded and a little uncomfortable.

"I'm sorry. I wasn't trying to be a snoop. The label caught my eye and I was curious."

She slipped the album from my hands. "It's OK," she said, but her tone implied it really wasn't.

"How did you get all those pictures of me?"

"Your grandmother sends me new ones of you and Gwenny every year."

"Really? She never talks about you. Gwenny and I were shocked to find out we even had an aunt."

Aunt Tilly glanced down at the peach sundress on her floor and cleared her throat again. "Nice choice," she said, changing the subject. "I'll see you downstairs." And, carrying the photo album, she left the room.

I stood there for a second feeling absolutely horrible. It wasn't like me to be nosy. And now it seemed I'd upset my aunt before I even got a chance to know her.

With a sigh, I went into my room and put the dress on, surprised with our size differences that it actually fit. I found a white scarf to tie my hair back, put my sandals back on, and headed downstairs.

Halfway down the stairs something out the window caught my attention and I turned to see Cade bent over a bush, pulling something from the ground. Although it was midmorning, his shirtless back glistened with sweat. My gaze trailed downward and I noticed he was wearing the same shorts as the day before.

I sighed and went the rest of the way into the kitchen.

"Well," Domino exclaimed. "Don't you look like a slice of pretty peach pie?"

I felt myself blush a little. Gwenny was the one who always got compliments on her looks, not me.

He put a plate down on the kitchen island. "Now, for the palate challenge." A soufflé sat centered on the dish, with a whole-wheat English muffin on the side. I eyed the beautiful breakfast, excited to get my taste buds popping.

Domino nodded anxiously toward the plate. "I hid a few things in that. Let's see what you got."

I took a seat on one of the barstools and eagerly pulled the plate over, picked up a fork, and took a small bite. "Egg whites, of course. Goat cheese, milk, butter, flour." I took another bite. "Table salt, not sea, and black pepper. Bread-crumb base." Another bite. "And just a dab of plain old Season-All. I'm pretty sure that's it." I looked up at him expectantly. "Well?"

He threw his dishtowel down and waved his oversized fork at me. "Girl, you are officially my challenge for the summer. I swear to God, I *will* stump you."

"And I'll look forward to having you try!"

Aunt Tilly pushed through the swinging door with a bucket and mop. "Doesn't that soufflé rock?"

"It does more than rock," I agreed.

She put the bucket down. "That dress fits you great."

"Thanks. And I am really sorry about the photo album, I just . . ."

She winked at me. "No need to apologize. All is forgotten."

I sighed with relief. But something still nagged at the back of my brain. Why had she seemed so taken off guard?

Cade strolled through the back archway and interrupted my thoughts. He breezed past me and over to the refrigerator where he got out a jug of orange juice, took a cup from the hanging rack, and poured himself a glass.

I tried really hard not to stare at his tanned chest as he drank it down in one long swallow.

He put the juice away, shook back his shaggy blond hair, and then looked right at me. Inwardly, I cursed, wishing I hadn't been caught staring at him. Outwardly, I went back to my breakfast as if I *hadn't* been looking.

"Is that Tilly's dress?" Cade asked.

"Yes. My luggage still hasn't arrived." I waited for him to say I looked nice, but he didn't.

"I thought Cade and Frederick could show you around the island tomorrow," my aunt offered. "Sound good?"

"Sure." I nodded and chanced a look at Cade.

He gave me a half-grin that shot butterflies right through my stomach.

"And today," she continued, "you can just hang out around here and see the goings-on."

"Sounds good."

With a smile, she went back to washing dishes, and Cade swept past me and out the back.

My cell phone buzzed and I checked the display. Gwenny! "It's my sister. I'm going to take it upstairs. Do you mind?"

Aunt Tilly waved me off. "Not at all."

"Hi!" I greeted Gwenny as I trotted up the back stairs.

"Hi! Hi! Hi! Hi! Hi!" she chirped back.

We both laughed.

"Oh my God," she whined, "you've been gone only one day and I desperately miss you."

Smiling, I flopped across my bed.

"Tell me everything," Gwenny encouraged excitedly, "and don't leave anything out."

I spent the next twenty minutes detailing everything.

"I can't believe we have a cousin."

"I know."

"And Cade sounds amazing."

I smiled at that. "Hey, did you know Grandmother's been sending Aunt Tilly pictures of you and me since we were little kids?"

"Really? And we didn't know we even had an aunt."

"That's what I said!" I rolled over onto my back and stuffed a pillow under my head. "It's really odd." I paused. "So, what's going on there?"

Gwenny sighed. "Nothing. Logan went away with his parents, so it's back to the usual. Boring. Want to bang my head against the wall. Grandmother's coming to dinner tomorrow night."

"Tell her I said hi."

"Yeah, yeah, yeah," she sarcastically droned. "Just make sure you have fun for both of us."

"I'll give it my best shot."

"And Em?"

"Yes?"

"Don't forget to try something new!"

I said bye to Gwenny and headed back downstairs and out the back door of the Pepper House. I stood for a few seconds taking in the sight of the bay, the cottages across it, and several sailboats slowly bobbing along in the water.

A tiny rocky beach marked my aunt's property at the water's edge and I headed toward it. I leaned down and picked up a rock. Rolling it around in my hand, I turned and looked back up at the Pepper House.

The two-story main building encompassed nearly half the property, its windows and shutters open to the island breeze. Gorgeous green trees with bright red flowers grew tall and lush. Off to the right and tucked in behind greenery sat one of the whitewashed cottages, and off to the left sat the other.

A wrought-iron fence ran the length of the property, separating it from the homes on the right and left of us.

I couldn't recall ever seeing anything so quaint, alluring, and beautiful. And to think I had a whole month to enjoy it all!

* * *

That afternoon, I sat in the great room across from my cousin studying the chessboard. I couldn't believe how good he was. A little *too* good, actually. Like competition-level good. It was a bit intimidating, as *I* was used to being the winner in a chess match. I hated to admit it, but in just a few more moves I was pretty sure he'd have me.

Frederick moved his queen forward one block.

I took one of his pawns in a diagonal sweep. "Who taught you how to play?"

"My dad," he answered.

"Is . . . is he around much?" I wasn't generally the type of person to pry into people's personal lives, but I was so very curious about my new family.

Frederick shook his head. "He died a long time ago."

"Oh." I didn't really know what else to say about that.

"It's OK," Frederick told me, as if reading my thoughts.

Across the room, the front door to the Pepper House opened and in stumbled a couple, both tall and lanky with bright red hair.

"The honeymooners," Frederick whispered.

Laughing hysterically, they clung to each other as they crossed the living room. The man mumbled something to the woman and they laughed even harder. Frederick and I watched in amusement as they continued on, not even noticing we were sitting in the corner.

Frederick turned back to the game. "They've been here a week and that's how they are every time I see them."

I smiled. That was exactly how I hoped to be with the guy I fell in love with.

Frederick moved his bishop three spaces diagonally—straight into the line of my knight. I studied the move, finding it odd, of course, that he was basically giving me a kill. I looked up at his face for any signs, but he held his expression poker flat. I searched the board, looking for an ulterior motive, and even though my gut said I shouldn't, I took his bishop with my knight.

He promptly took my knight with his rook.

My jaw dropped. How had I missed that?

Aunt Tilly picked that moment to whirl in. "Oh, there you two are!"

She came over and stroked one hand over Frederick's head and the other over mine. "Who's winning?"

I pointed to Frederick. "You've got quite the genius here."

She winked. "Runs in the family. So," she looked over to me, "I saw a cookbook in your room . . . ?"

An alarm went off in my head, and I immediately squashed it. This was Tilly, not my mom. "Oh, yeah, it's sort of a hobby."

"Hm, I suspected as much." She studied me for a second. "How about I talk to Domino? See about you helping out in the kitchen?"

I perked up. "Really?"

She laughed. "Really."

I smiled at Frederick with a grin I felt sure showed every bit of excitement bubbling inside me.

He chuckled. "You must really like cooking."

"I do!" Immediately I thought of Navia. "I've made so many wonderful dishes over the years with Navia, our housekeeper. She's a fabulous teacher. She taught me how to mix and mingle the things you'd least expect to allow true flavors to come out. She used to play this blindfold game with me when I was a kid, seeing if I could recognize what she was putting in my mouth." I laughed as I remembered. "One time she put a black bean stuffed in a Greek olive, sure the brine from the olive would mask the bean, but I caught her! I totally tasted the bean."

I grinned at Frederick and Aunt Tilly and they both smiled back in this sort of puzzled way.

Frederick chuckled again. "Yeah, you really do like cooking."

I felt myself warm in embarrassment at my exuberant display, but I didn't care. I didn't have to hide my excitement of cooking here. And that made me feel so wonderful I nearly wanted to shout.

Aunt Tilly leaned down and kissed the top of my head. "Anything that makes you that happy is definitely worth exploring."

I let out a contented sigh. She was right, it *was* worth exploring. I was completely free here. Free to do things that made me truly happy.

Chapter Six

The front door opened and Cade strode in with a giggling girl hanging on his arm. The girl was pretty. *Really* pretty. Short like me but with every feature opposite. Fair skin instead of my olive tone. Cropped dark hair in lieu of my long. Very thin. And although she was dressed just about as sloppily as they came, in cutoff jean shorts and a white tank top, somehow it made her even cuter.

Cade poked her in the ribs, bringing out more laughter between them, and I squashed a pang of jealousy that came out of nowhere. Why in the world would I be jealous?

The girl glanced up, caught sight of me and Frederick, and shot us a huge grin. "Hi! You must be Elizabeth Margaret."

I couldn't help but smile back. Her extroverted personality reminded me of Aunt Tilly.

The girl bounced over to us and held out her hand. "I'm Beth. I'm the Domestic Engineer here."

I shook her hand. "Oh, I've heard all about you. It's nice to meet you."

"Oh, no," she joked, "the family's been yapping, have they?"

I chuckled. "No, nothing like that."

Beth turned and gave Frederick an affectionate knuckle rub on the head, and he batted her hand away. She was twenty-one, I remembered Aunt Tilly saying. But looking at her, she could've easily passed for my age.

"So, have you met everybody?" she asked.

I nodded. "I think so."

"You're going to love it here, Elizabeth Margaret. You've landed in quite the paradise for the summer. Maybe you and I can grab dinner out sometime. I know a lot of cute guys I can introduce you to."

"Sure. That'd be great."

"Elizabeth Margaret," she mumbled my name, looking into the air. "That's a mouthful. We should come up with a nickname for you. Lizzie, Maggie . . ."

"Actually, my sister calls me Em." I was surprised at how easily that suggestion came after a lifetime of being called my full name by everyone *but* my sister.

"Em." Beth gave one affirmative nod. "I like it."

"Me too," Frederick agreed.

We all glanced at Cade. "Em it is."

Beth waved good-bye to everybody. "I'm off to work. Nice

meeting ya!" And with that, she bounded out of the living room.

I glanced at Frederick, who had his attention glued back to the chessboard.

Cade grabbed a chair. "So who's winning?"

I rolled my eyes to my cousin and Cade smiled. "Sounds about right."

He scooted in close to see the game and I found myself staring at him. His blond hair, a little stubble along his jaw from where he hadn't shaved, and a muscle moving in his cheek where he was chewing a piece of gum.

Around his neck hung a tiny gold ring. I looked at it, suddenly remembering I'd seen it in the pictures of him in my aunt's album. He must have felt me staring because he quietly tucked the ring inside his T-shirt.

"I saw some pictures of you two," I told them.

"Oh yeah?" Cade shifted in his seat and his knee brushed mine.

I swallowed, all my attention suddenly very preoccupied by our touching knees. "Um, in Tilly's album. You two must have grown up together?"

Frederick and Cade exchanged a glance. "Pretty much," my cousin said. "Cade's the closest thing to a brother that I have."

"Yeah, actually, I lived here at the Pepper House for several years."

"You did?" I looked between the two guys. "What about your parents?"

"Oh, they barely missed me." Cade pushed back from the

table, and I immediately missed the feeling of his knee. "Well, I've got tons of work to do. Catch you two later." And with that, he was gone.

I sat there a second, wondering what had just happened. "Did I say something wrong?"

Frederick swept his queen across the board and took my king. "Checkmate."

I didn't bother pointing out the fact he hadn't given me a proper "Check" notice first. "Next time you're mine," I joked.

My cousin started resetting the pieces. "You didn't say anything wrong. Cade's had a lot of issues with his parents. He doesn't like to talk about it."

"Oh." I helped Frederick put the pieces back on the board, wondering what problems Cade had had. I hoped it wasn't anything too terrible.

"So where did you see these pictures?"

"In an album your mom has in her closet."

Frederick nodded. "She's got lots of them."

"Did you know Grandmother has been sending her pictures of me and Gwenny for years?"

"Yep. Just like she sends Grandmother pictures of me."

"Then why didn't I know about you guys?"

Frederick laughed at my exasperation and shrugged. "All I know is that Grandmother and my mom have never gotten along. They've done nothing but fight their whole lives."

"Yet they send each other pictures?"

My cousin shrugged, as clueless as me.

"Do you ever hear from Grandmother?"

Frederick stepped his knight over a pawn. "I get a card on my birthday and at Christmas."

I paused. "Do you all send us stuff?"

He nodded. "Obviously you've never gotten it, though. Otherwise you would've known about us."

I studied him, thinking back over the years. Why would my parents hide birthday cards, Christmas cards, and whatever else? *Why?*

* * *

The next afternoon my suitcase arrived and I unpacked the boring clothes that my mom always insisted I wear. They had no fun or flair. And after wearing items from my aunt's wonderful carefree wardrobe, I realized even more how staid my old clothes were.

A half hour later I crossed through the kitchen and a savory smell had me glancing in the oven. Pot roast simmered in a big pan. I checked the thermometer, assuring it was edible, and got a fork from the drawer. I sampled a bit of the meat, decided it needed thyme, and found some dried in a ziplock.

I didn't care for dried herbs, and was surprised they didn't have fresh, but the roast definitely needed thyme. I sprinkled it over the top and prayed Domino wouldn't mind too much.

I noticed then he didn't have the accompanying vegetables prepped. Some carrots, onion, new potatoes.

I dug around in the refrigerator and pantry and found what I needed. I lit a flame under a sauté pan and drizzled in grapeseed oil and some red wine. I threw in some chunked garlic and bubbled it around. Chopped yellow onion came next, and while it simmered I quartered the potatoes and julienne sliced the large carrots.

The trick, as Navia had taught me, was to just get the vegetables tender, then situate them on top the roast, not letting them fall into the liquid. Some tented and ventilated aluminum foil over the whole thing, and it all would come out perfect hours later.

Frederick stepped from the back archway and into the kitchen. "Wow, something smells good."

I started washing up the stuff I'd dirtied. "Pot roast."

"Did you make it?"

"No. I added a few things, though." I glanced at my cousin. "You don't think Domino will mind, do you?"

Frederick shrugged. "Beats me. It smells so good, I doubt it."

"I hope not." I dried off my hands. "Hey, I was hoping to see the cottages. They're empty, right?"

He nodded. "We've got some people checking in tonight, though."

"Perfect. And then sightseeing?"

"You bet!"

My cousin and I headed through the dining room, out the side door, and down the pebbled path toward one of the cottages.

More of that fantastic greenery with the huge red flowers lined the path. To the right stretched the bay and to the left a tall trellis separated the grounds from the driveway. I glanced through the lattice and saw that the van was there, which meant Cade was probably around somewhere too.

The path led straight to a stone cottage that looked like a miniature version of the main house. The door sat open. I peeked my head in. "Hello?"

"Back here," someone yelled, and I realized it was Beth.

I stepped into a cozy living room with a huge window that overlooked the bay. A painting hung on the wall. Its realistic, colorful depiction reminded me of the one hanging in my room and the others I'd seen scattered around the Pepper House. This one showed a young couple riding bikes along a cliff. Laughing, the couple extended their arms, trying to touch fingers as they sped along the road. Like before, I found myself wanting to crawl right in and participate in the fun.

"Hey," Beth said from behind me and I turned around. Cade stood beside her.

"Hey," I greeted her back.

Wearing rubber gloves and holding a rag, she nodded to the painting. "Isn't it great?"

"It's more than great. I've seen more of this same work around the house. I've been meaning to ask Tilly who the artist is."

She shrugged. "Dunno," she said, and looked at Cade. "Any idea?"

He shook his head and crossed over to where his toolbox sat on the floor.

I turned back to the painting. "Well, whoever it is, he or she is very talented. They're amazing."

"Yeah, very alive with energy," Beth agreed.

"There's lots more of this artist's work around the island,"

Frederick said. "You'll see when we go sightseeing."

We all looked at the painting a few seconds longer and then Beth turned and looked at me. She checked out my green plaid shorts and matching polo shirt. "Your suitcase came."

I nodded at the obvious.

"You look nice."

"Thanks."

Cade closed his toolbox and latched the lid. "Speaking of sightseeing. You guys ready?"

I smiled. "Definitely!" And looked at Beth. "Coming?"

She waved us off. "You guys have fun. I'm going to finish things up here."

"All right," Cade said with a nod. "Let's go."

Chapter Seven

Cade, Frederick, and I headed out front and climbed in the van. Cade cranked the engine, and we pulled away from the Pepper House onto the coastal highway.

"So what's the game plan?" I asked.

"We're going to cruise the coast," Cade answered.

"Then show you around downtown," Frederick put in.

"And whatever else," Cade continued. "Just yell if you see anything you want to look at, and we'll stop. Cool?"

I smiled. "Cool." I turned and took in the ocean sparkling out my passenger-side window. I closed my eyes and heard the wind as it flowed in, the seagulls squawking, and the ocean lapping against the shore. "Gorgeous," I sighed.

"Nature at its purest and most wonderful," Cade agreed.

I turned and looked at him, surprised he'd said something so insightful.

"Great diving," Cade added, pointing past me.

Roughly fifty feet off the shore were giant boulders towering out of the ocean. I caught sight of snorkels bobbing in the water as people floated belly-down, staring at the underwater sights.

I'd been snorkeling many times, but never diving. "You certified?" I asked him.

He nodded.

I turned back to Frederick. "You?"

"Nah, but I can snorkel with the best of them."

"I've always been sort of afraid of scuba diving," I admitted.

Cade glanced at me. "Why's that?"

I shrugged. "It just seems so far down."

"It's not so bad," he said, glancing off to the right.

I followed his line of sight to see a small marina coming into view. It stretched into the ocean and was bracketed in on three sides by a natural rocky barrier. I counted twenty boats in all.

"You mind if we stop? Gwenny loves sailing. I should get some pictures for her."

Cade didn't answer me at first as he stared hard at the marina and attached parking lot.

"Cade?"

He brought his eyes to mine. "Um, yeah, if you want."

He pulled the van in and parked it near a small wooden building with OFFICE printed across the door. There were only four vehicles in the parking lot, all rusted by the salt spray.

Frederick slid the side door open. "Anybody want drinks?"

I nodded, getting out. "Sure. Something lemon-lime for me."

"I'm fine," Cade replied.

As my cousin went over to the drink machine, I headed down the dock. When I was a few boats in, I realized Cade hadn't followed. I turned to see him still sitting in the van, watching me.

You coming? I mouthed, and he shook his head.

I turned back to the dock and continued on, passing mostly sailboats. There were small ones, big ones. Some well cared for, others decrepit. Quite a few had to have people living on them, from the looks of the outdoor carpeting and potted plants, and moss growing on the sides. And a few more were obvious transits with their foreign flags flying and owners doing minor repairs.

With my phone, I snapped off a few pictures and sent them to Gwenny.

At the end of the dock towered a powerboat I guessed to be one hundred feet in length. A large man stood with his feet braced apart and a tight shirt stretched over his bulging muscles. Even though dark glasses hid his eyes, I got the distinct impression he was watching me.

"Hello," I greeted him, eyeing the monstrous boat behind him.

"No further, miss, this is a private area."

I nodded. "Of course. Have a good afternoon." I turned back around, more than curious who was on that boat. A movie star? A politician?

Halfway back down the dock, I heard, "Wouldn't let you on, would he?"

I turned to the right, where a sailboat floated. I guessed it to be about thirty-five feet. With its hammock tied between two masts, canvases stretched for shade, and homey feel, I assumed the person lived on it.

A tall skinny man with long blond hair and sun-leathered skin nodded at me. I guessed him to be around forty. He had one of those pooched bellies that came from too much beer.

I held my hand up to shade the sun from my eyes as I looked up at him. "Hello."

"Wouldn't let you on?" he asked again.

"Oh, I didn't want to go on. He did tell me to turn around, though." I glanced back at the huge powerboat. "Any idea who's on it?"

"It just pulled in yesterday. There've only been workers out and about." The man ran his fingers through his hair, smoothing it into a ponytail, and then wrapped a rubber band around it.

"Well," I said, starting off, "better get back."

"You here on vacation?" he asked, stopping me.

"Yes, sir."

He laughed at that. "I can't recall the last time someone called me sir."

I smiled a little.

He gestured up the dock to where the van still sat with Cade behind the wheel and Frederick now back inside. "Staying at the Pepper House?"

"Yes, my aunt owns it."

The man smiled and I saw he was missing some teeth. He seemed too young to be missing teeth. "Let me guess: Elizabeth Margaret?"

He laughed at my surprised expression. "Small island," he followed up in explanation.

I didn't know if that was a good or bad thing, everyone knowing one another's business.

"I'm Sid, by the way."

"Nice to meet you, Sid."

He glanced back up the dock. "Well, you oughta get. I'm sure Cade is up there waitin'. You come back sometime for a visit if you like. Maybe I'll know who's on that boat by then."

I knew I'd just met the man, but a visit with him did sound like an intriguing idea. I'd always wondered about people who lived on sailboats. What kind of life they lived, their stories, how they came to live that way, what they did for a living . . .

As I thought all these questions over, I found my way back up the dock.

"I see you met Sid," Cade said as I opened the van door and climbed in.

I nodded. "He seems like an OK guy."

Cade made a noncommittal grunt.

I looked over my shoulder at Frederick, who'd become inordinately focused on his soda. OK, what was going on here?

Cade put the van in gear and slowly pulled out of the parking lot.

I glanced out my open window and down the dock to

where Sid still stood in the same spot on his boat, watching us drive off. "You two know each other?"

"Yeah, you could say that." Cade shifted gears and pushed on the gas pedal. "Just do me a favor? Stay clear of him." He accelerated down the coastal highway, picking up speed, and passed a couple of bikes. "He's not a very nice man."

Chapter Eight

C ade cranked on his reggae music, making it more than clear he wasn't talking any more on the subject of Sid.

As soon as we got back to the Pepper House, I was definitely going to ask Aunt Tilly about the man on the sailboat and why, exactly, Cade had warned me to stay away.

We completed the tour of the coastline, and Cade turned off onto a narrow paved road covered on both sides by thick greenery and a multitude of colored flowers. Through the greenery I made out cottages, much like the two my aunt rented out.

"Some of the island's older families live in those," Cade commented, turning the music down.

The narrow road opened onto a hillside covered in

rectangular aboveground stone graves. Nearly every grave looked well tended with fresh flowers. I'd seen graves like this before in some of my travels with my parents, but the sight always gave me goose bumps.

Frederick leaned up from the backseat. "It's strange, but I've always liked graveyards."

I looked back. "Me, too. It's the—"

"History," my cousin finished for me. "Isn't it amazing the names, the relations, how they died . . . ?" Frederick's voice trailed off as he pondered the headstones.

And I thought I was the only graveyard freak in the family.

"You two are weird," Cade said, rolling forward in the van.

Frederick and I exchanged a smile, and he nodded out the front window. "Don't miss this."

I turned as we peaked the hillside, and I caught my breath. "Oh my gosh, that view is amazing."

Cade turned the music off, and we sat in the idling van, staring out over the entire island. In all directions to the horizon spanned the vibrant blue ocean. Green covered every inch. Trees, bushes, ivy, plants in every shade imaginable.

Tucked in here and there were stone cottages and buildings, some tiny, others medium-sized, and yet others like the Pepper House with lots of space and outbuildings.

A number of small bays, like the one near my aunt's place, cut into the island. Smack dab in the center sat a cluster of colorful buildings that I assumed to be the historical township. And all the way to my right sprawled a huge resort, looking so out of place and dominating in this unique setting.

I saw no roads and could only assume they were hidden by

the lush greenery. Straight across I made out the marina where Sid and his boat floated and, to the right, the airport.

Smiling, I sighed contentedly. "This place reminds me of Bermuda."

"Any further out into the Atlantic and it would be Bermuda," Frederick said.

Cade put the van in gear and started down the hill. "Let's go see our big metropolis."

I laughed a little at his humor.

Minutes later we drove into town. The number of people on the streets surprised me. From our hilltop view, it had appeared as though the place sat empty, but now I could see that the island had a thriving tourist trade.

Myriad shops lined the cobblestone streets, all mom-and-pop, family-owned places—restaurants, clothing stores, knickknack sellers, and a variety of others. I saw no chain establishments. I liked it that way. It gave it an old-world feeling—how things must have been a century ago before big corporations took over.

"You'll find none of your fancy designer stuff here," Cade joked.

"Hey . . ." His comment struck me. Is that how he viewed me? All snobby fashionista? I did have a lot of designer clothes, but my mom did most of the shopping for Gwenny and me. If I had my way, well, I wasn't sure what my style would be.

I glanced down at my plaid shorts and coordinating polo, suddenly embarrassed. I wished I had on another one of my aunt's flowy dresses.

Giggles had me gazing out the front windshield, where a pack of girls I guessed to be thirteen or fourteen had gathered outside an ice-cream shop.

"*Hiii,* Cade," one flirted, and all the others giggled again.

Cade gave them a small smile and wave.

"Aren't they a little young for you?" I teased.

"He gets that everywhere we go," Frederick grumbled.

Heck, I'd probably giggle too, if I were thirteen again. That half-grin thing he had going on was definitely swoon-worthy.

Cade pulled the van over and cut the engine. He opened his door and jumped out. "You guys going to be OK? I got a few things to do."

"Sure," Frederick answered, sliding open the side door. "Meet you at the art gallery in an hour."

I watched Cade stroll away, wishing more than I should that he would be joining me and Frederick.

Frederick motioned between two buildings. "We'll head this way and then cut across to Key Street. That's where the tourists always hit when they come. Not so much us locals, but you've got to have your share of the touristy thing."

Frederick cut off into a store and I followed.

"So what's up with Sid?" I asked. "Why doesn't Cade want me around him?"

"Mmmm . . . it's not really my thing to tell. Cade's right, though. You should probably stay away from him."

I sighed. "It's all very mysterious."

My cousin laughed. "Not really. Just family stuff."

"Family. Seems like that's the theme of this summer." I picked a conch shell up off a shelf and idly studied it. "Ya know, cuz, I think you and my sister would really get along. It's a shame we didn't all grow up together."

He looked at me. "Yeah, it is. Maybe things can be different now that you and I know each other."

"Maybe," I agreed, but I didn't see how. Not with my parents, grandmother, and Tilly barely talking.

We spent the next thirty minutes or so weaving in and out of stores, meeting the locals, and enjoying the laid-back vibe.

To my surprise, nearly every person knew who I was and that I'd be there for half the summer. I felt very at home. As if I'd been missing this small-town camaraderie my entire life.

As the hour and the afternoon drew to an end, Frederick led me into the last store on Key Street, a gallery of paintings and sculptures. He headed over to look at a new display of Civil War paintings, and I meandered through the remaining three rooms, appreciating the artistry.

I took a slow walk around the last room, rounded a display case of scrimshaw, and came face-to-face with a painting I knew was by the same artist who had done the ones hanging in the Pepper House.

I'd never really been into the specifics of brushstrokes, pastels, oils, and canvases, but I could appreciate art with the best of them. And I could honestly say no art had ever drawn me in like these paintings did.

I wasn't sure if it was the whirl of colors, the real-life depiction, or the honesty in the people's faces. All I knew was that the paintings moved me. They spoke to my heart. Whoever this artist was, he or she had an amazing talent.

"May I help you?" a lady asked from behind me.

I turned. "Who painted this?"

She smiled. "A local artist."

I turned back to the painting, smiling at the preteen couple as they held hands and leapt from a cliff into the water below. I could almost hear their laughter.

"You ready?" Cade asked, and I glanced past the woman to where he stood with Frederick behind him.

I pointed to the painting. "Isn't this incredible?"

Cade gave it a cursory glance. "It's all right, I guess, if you're into that sort of thing." He headed toward the exit. "Meet you guys outside."

I turned to the lady when Cade was gone. "Thank you. Your gallery is lovely."

She nodded. "You come back anytime."

Minutes later I was back in the van, Cade's music was on, and we were on our way home. Sticking my arm out the window, I rode the wind with my hand, loving the warmth and sense of freedom that a hand out the window gave. I promised myself I would savor every second of this wonderful month with my new family. I wouldn't take anything for granted.

After a little while we pulled up to the Pepper House.

Domino glanced up as we walked into the kitchen. "You put thyme in my roast, didn't you, sweetie?"

I grimaced. "I did. And made vegetables, too. Sorry."

He frowned. "Sorry? Are you kidding me? It's exactly what it needed."

"Em, it was absolutely awesome!" Beth said from where she was sitting on a barstool.

I smiled. "Really?"

"Everybody loved it." Domino waggled his spoon at me. "I want you down here first thing in the morning. Your aunt told me cooking is your hobby. Can't say I'm surprised, given that palate of yours. But let's see how much of a hobby it is. You are now officially my sous chef."

My smile got even bigger. "Really?" I couldn't think of anything better.

Domino nodded. "And I'm giving you a new challenge. You wow me over the next week and I'll let you plan and make Sunday's brunch two weeks from now."

Was he for real? "B-but . . . ."

"'B-but,'" Domino mimicked me. "No buts. I know you've got it in you."

I shot a helpless look at Frederick, who held up his hands. "Don't look at me."

Beth slid off the barstool. "It'll be fun. We can go to the farmers' market the day before and buy everything."

But I had to wow Domino first.

"Mmm," Beth mumbled approvingly, "and we've got the best fresh fish."

Fresh fish? My mind started to drift as I thought of all the possibilities . . . dill haddock, Irish cod, planked salmon . . .

Cade snatched a brownie off a plate that sat on the center island. "Uh-oh. Watch out. I see her wheels turning."

If I did the salmon I could make sour cream and caviar sauce . . .

Aunt Tilly swung through the kitchen doors. "Wow, the whole family's here."

"Em's making Sunday brunch!" Beth announced.

Tilly glanced at Domino. "*You're* letting someone else make our Sunday brunch?"

Domino shrugged. "Two weeks from now. What can I say? I'm feeling generous. But that's *only* if she proves she can handle it. I've made her my sous chef."

Aunt Tilly turned a surprised look to me. "Sous chef? How cool are you?" She turned back to Domino with an affirmative nod. "She can handle it."

"And we're going to the farmers' market the Saturday before to buy everything," Beth continued.

"Farmers' market?" Aunt Tilly perked up. "I'm in. I've been so busy around here I haven't had a chance to visit our market in probably a month."

"I wonder if they have fresh lemongrass at this farmers' market," I said. "Also, I need to know my budget and how many people to expect."

Domino laughed. "We'll get to that. First, plan on making me the meal beforehand so I can approve it."

"Sounds good. I have a lot of work to do. I need to research white-wine reduction sauces and do some trial runs on oils to seal in the moisture of the fish. I might be up all night." Excitement danced around inside me as I thought of it all.

Frederick grabbed a brownie from the same plate Cade had. "Well, I was going to challenge you to a game of chess, but clearly you're preoccupied."

I gave him a sorry look. He was right. I was completely preoccupied. "Rain check?"

He took a bite of the brownie. "Sure."

"You're terribly cute when you're focused," Tilly teased.

I glanced at Cade, and he smiled and took a huge bite of the brownie. "Sounds like you're going to be very busy."

"Sounds like." Maybe it was my imagination, but he seemed a little bummed at that.

Beth headed toward the door. "Later, everybody. Cade, when you get a chance, I need help moving furniture."

He followed Beth out the door, and Aunt Tilly turned to me. "So, how was sightseeing? What did you guys do?"

"Oh, it was fun." I recapped everything we'd done from the marina to the hilltop to visiting downtown. "By the way, who is Sid?"

The whole kitchen got quiet. Frederick looked at Domino, who glanced at Aunt Tilly, who slowly reached for a brownie.

She cleared her throat. "You met Sid?"

I nodded, more than curious what was going on. "And I asked Frederick, but he won't give me the scoop."

I waited while they all exchanged looks again.

Aunt Tilly sighed and put the brownie back down. "Sid is Cade's dad. He's been gone for over a year. But"—Aunt Tilly paused and looked at Domino—"I guess he's back in town."

Chapter Nine

A little bit before sunset, Aunt Tilly and I each grabbed a bike and pedaled to a nearby beach. I'd thought a lot about Sid and Cade and wondered what had kept Sid away for more than a year.

I couldn't imagine my dad taking off for that long. In fact, he hardly ever went anywhere, except on family vacations with all of us.

"Biking has always been one of my favorite things to do," my aunt said, jarring me from my thoughts. She got off her bike to walk it through some thick sand. "Your mom and I actually used to ride bikes together a lot when we were younger."

"Mom used to ride a bike?" I took my flip-flops off and tossed them in my bike basket, excited she'd brought up family. "I find that hard to believe. I can't imagine Mom doing anything except be on her BlackBerry."

Aunt Tilly sighed. "I know. Things change over time."

"Did you and my mom do a lot of things together?"

Aunt Tilly climbed back on her bike and started off down the beach. "We did. You know, there're ten years between us, so we had our own set of friends and all that. But Kat was always so good about letting me tag along."

"Really?" I couldn't see my mom being so nice. "Did you just call her Kat?"

"It was always Kat when we were young, but when she got older, she went by Katherine. She's the one who started calling me Tilly." With the setting sun, Tilly propped her sunglasses on top of her head. "She used to get me ready for school in the morning. She'd brush my hair. I had such long hair, she'd curse it for the tangles." Aunt Tilly smiled. "I remember one time she twisted my braids around my ears and all the kids at school teased me that I looked like Princess Leia from *Star Wars*."

"Oh, that must have been a sight!" I laughed.

Aunt Tilly smiled, and then pointed to some surfers. "Ever been?"

"What, surfing? No."

"Cade surfs. You should ask him to give you a lesson."

My stomach swirled in excitement at that thought, imagining Cade and me spending time together. In the water. Alone.

"Your mom helped me build a doll house out of cardboard," my aunt interrupted my Cade daydream. "And she taught me how to wear makeup. When I had slumber parties, she'd go out and rent movies and get junk food for us."

Quietly, I listened, imagining all the things she was describing. Their relationship sounded close, like Gwenny and me. I couldn't help but wonder what caused them to grow so far apart.

Tilly waved to some people on the beach. "When she went away to college it was just your grandmother and me and, well, I don't think Grandmother really knew what to do with me."

We reached the pier and turned around. The sun was just disappearing into the horizon and I snapped off a quick picture of it. FOR YOU, I typed to Gwenny, and sent her the pic.

Smiling, I slipped my phone back into my pocket. "How often did Mom come home to visit?"

"Just on holidays mostly."

"I bet you really missed her."

Tilly nodded. "I did, but then she got busy and I started getting in trouble. The years rolled by, and here we all are." She glanced over at me then, studying me, like she was trying to decide if she wanted to say something that was on her mind.

"What?" I quietly asked.

Tilly turned her attention back to the sand in front of her. "Did you know your grandfather passed away the day I was born?"

I was speechless.

"He died in a car accident rushing to the hospital to be with your grandmother and me."

"I-I had no idea."

"Your grandmother loved him dearly and was absolutely lost without him. She went into a deep depression, so your mom took care of me from pretty much day one."

"Poor Grandmother." My heart sank at the thought of what she must have gone through. A brand-new baby. A dead husband. "Do you think she blamed you? Is that why you don't get along?"

Tilly mulled that question over for a second. "Maybe she blamed me. She's never said as much, but maybe somewhere deep inside her she did."

We pedaled in silence for a few minutes, lost in our thoughts. I wondered why my mom had never told me about my grandfather's death. Maybe Grandmother asked her not to.

"So what eventually brought you here?" I asked my aunt.

She pointed up the beach to the path that we'd first come down. "That's for another time. I think I'm talked out for the night," she said, smiling.

I nodded and followed her back to the Pepper House.

An hour or so later I sat in the dimly lit kitchen, sipping some cranberry juice, thinking about my family. I had tried to call Gwenny when we first got back, but she didn't answer. I couldn't wait to hear what she thought about everything.

Aunt Tilly was in her office doing paperwork and Frederick was upstairs reading.

I opened my cookbook and leafed through it.

My phone beeped and I looked at the caller ID. How fitting that my mom interrupted me right as I'd opened my cookbook—like she knew or something. I hit the speaker button and turned the volume low. "Hello, Mom."

"Elizabeth Margaret, how are you?"

"Fine," I answered.

"What have you been doing with your days?"

"Sightseeing, hanging out, relaxing . . ." Getting ready to be a sous chef, I wanted to add, but I knew she wouldn't like that response.

"Matilda isn't making you work, is she?"

Making me? No. But I had been because I wanted to. "No, Mom, Aunt Tilly isn't making me work."

"Because you're not there as hired help." Mom's voice got a little snappish. "Just because she runs a B&B and you're family doesn't mean you owe her anything. If she asks you to work for your room and board, well, you just come back home."

I sighed in frustrated confusion. "Aunt Tilly doesn't want me to work for room and board, Mom. Why would you think that? In fact, she's done nothing *but* encourage me to relax."

Silence. "Oh, well, good then. That's as it should be."

I rolled my eyes, wishing Gwenny were here to share my annoyance.

"And you're acting like a lady? You haven't done anything to be ashamed of?"

"What? Seriously?" I shook my head in disgust. I didn't understand my mom sometimes.

Cade walked in then and headed over to the refrigerator. I nodded hello, took my phone off speaker, and turned my back.

"No," I lowered my voice, "I haven't done anything to be ashamed of. Mom, would you relax? Why are you asking me such ridiculous questions?"

Silence.

Sometimes I wish I could just hang up on my mom. Or walk away from a room she occupied. I knew if I did, though, I'd never hear the end of it.

"Has . . . Matilda talked about our family?"

"A little. She told me about Grandfather's death. And she also shared some stories about the two of you. Mom, it sounds like you two were very close at one time. What happened?"

She didn't have a response to that.

"Mom?"

"I need to go," she hurriedly replied. "Your father sends his love."

"Tell him hi for me," I muttered, and heard her click off.

Cade put his glass in the sink. "I'm done for the night. Mind telling Tilly I'm out of here?"

"OK." I paused. "Um, how much of that did you hear?"

He shrugged. "A little."

I grabbed my phone and turned the power off, more to give my hands something to do than anything else. "She's not that bad," I halfheartedly defended my mom.

"Mm-hm," he agreed.

My eyes darted to his. "What's that mean?"

He shook his head. "I didn't say anything. All I said was mm-*hm*."

"Well, that was a loaded mm-*hm*," I snapped, not really

knowing why. Maybe I just needed to take my irritation out on somebody.

Cade shrugged. "Listen, she's your mom. And I only heard a little of the conversation. I don't know anything. OK?"

"That's right," I quickly came back at him. "You don't know anything—about me or my mom. Just like I don't know anything about your dad."

Cade's entire body visibly tensed and my heart began to thud deep and slow. I knew I'd just taken things too far.

Quiet seconds passed as we stared at each other across the kitchen.

"You're right," he very deliberately spoke. "You don't know anything about Sid. So stay out of my business and I'll stay out of yours."

And with that, he was gone.

I closed my cookbook and sat there as tears welled up in my eyes. I didn't know what was going on anymore. My family was turning out to be a complete mystery to me and now Cade was pissed off and totally had a right to be. I felt lost and out of focus.

I got up and started to rummage through the pantry, pulling out flour, sugar, vanilla, and baking powder. Since Gwenny wasn't around to talk, the next best thing for me to do was bake. I'm not necessarily a great baker, but even a bad sugar cookie was still a sugar cookie, and it would allow me to bury my confusion and sadness in a bowl of dough.

* * *

The next morning (three dozen sugar cookies later) dawned bright and beautiful—my first official morning as Domino's sous chef. I should have been more excited than I was, but my disagreement with Cade had definitely left me moody.

I had a few minutes until I needed to be in the kitchen and so I dialed Gwenny's number.

She picked up on the fourth ring. "Do you have any idea what time it is?" she groaned.

"Yes, it's six in the morning," I informed her, knowing full well she was a total grouch when she first woke up.

"I was having the most amazing dream about some dark-haired pirate and me sailing off into the sunset. And we were *just about to kiss* when you called and woke me up."

"Sorry," I dutifully apologized. "But . . . I've been baking all night."

"Oh, what's wrong?"

I told her all about my bike ride with Tilly and everything she'd said.

"Wow," Gwenny responded. "That's awful what happened to Grandmother."

"I know."

"I bet you're right. I bet she secretly blamed Tilly for Grandfather's death and that's why they've never gotten along."

"But it doesn't explain why Tilly and Mom don't get along. I feel like our family is one big mystery. I'll have to do some more digging and see if I can find out more." I paused. "And then there's my other problem. I think I pissed off Cade."

"Oh? The cute boy? What did you do?"

I told her what happened.

"Oh, Em. You need to apologize. I'm sure he'll forgive you."

"I don't know. I think I really touched a nerve." I looked down at my watch. "Ooh, I gotta go. I'm due down in the kitchen for sous-chef duty."

"Oh my God, you are so in your element right now. Let me know what happens. Especially with Cade."

"I will. Bye!"

I shut my phone, ran downstairs, and entered the kitchen, where Domino handed me an apron with *Pepper House* embroidered on it. In the top right corner *Em* had been stitched in. I smiled.

Domino nodded to the sink. "Wash up and then start prepping by chopping that basil. We're making spiced turkey cakes with stuffed tomatoes, artichoke dill salad, and strawberry-banana shakes for dessert."

"Yum, that sounds good."

Domino waved his spoon in the air. "I bought the turkey yesterday and ground it with just a teeny bit of chicken thigh. That's the key to the richness."

I slid a knife from the block and started chopping. "Navia, our housekeeper, has these exact knives. They're great."

"Is she a good cook?"

"The best. I learned a lot from her."

Domino opened the refrigerator and got out a container of yogurt. "I bet you were in the kitchen all the time helping her whip up things."

"I was—when no one was around to catch me."

He glanced at me. "What do you mean?"

I shrugged. "Nothing, just that my mother would get upset if I helped her. It was her job, not mine. She was getting paid to cook, not me."

"How's your mom going to feel about you being in here helping me?"

I gave him a look. "I don't know. I don't plan on telling her."

"Ah, a secret, I see."

I started chopping the basil. Domino held up a knife. "I special ordered these knives ten years ago," Domino said, continuing the previous conversation. "I wouldn't cut with anything less."

"Ten years ago? That's when Aunt Tilly said she bought this place."

Domino spooned vanilla yogurt into the blender. "Actually, she inherited Pepper House."

I glanced up at him. "Inherited?"

He plopped a banana and some strawberries on top of the yogurt and hit the On button. "Yeah, she worked here as a maid, learned her way around things, got familiar with the books, was an assistant to the owner, et cetera. And when the owner died, he left it to her."

"He left this *whole* place to Aunt Tilly?"

Domino nodded and hit the Off button. "Yep."

I started in on the garlic and parsley next. "What about you, Domino? How long have you worked here?"

"I was here before your aunt." He poured the shake from

the blender and put a small glass in front of me. "And when she inherited the place, she wrote me in as her partner on the deed."

I glanced up. "So you guys own this place together?"

"That's right." Domino put a glass bowl in front of me. It was already filled with the rest of the ingredients. "Put your choppings in here, mix it together with the turkey, and shape out twenty patties. I'll start in on coring the tomatoes."

We worked side by side, almost in sync, reading each other's minds and naturally falling into a smooth rhythm. I felt like I was starting to fit in. And I couldn't recall ever having felt that way before. I'd lived seventeen years doing everything I was supposed to *in order to* fit in but never quite feeling as though I'd succeeded. And now, in only a few days, I had a whole new feeling about my life.

I smiled over at Domino. He didn't know it, but being in this kitchen had already changed me. And I couldn't wait to do it all over again tomorrow.

* * *

I sat on my bed, my cookbook open to a recipe for a lamb dish. Almost a week had gone by since my disagreement with Cade, and I'd barely seen him since. I'd catch him pulling weeds in Aunt Tilly's yard, shuffling stuff around in the outdoor shed, or eating late in the kitchen. But every time I saw him he was alone, and every time I tried to speak to him, he found some excuse to walk off.

His silence bothered me. Maybe more than it should have,

but I found that I couldn't help myself. I felt so bad about how things had gone. If we could rewind things, I would have handled that last conversation differently. I wouldn't have gotten so irritated and snappy. And I certainly wouldn't have brought up Sid.

"Hey." Frederick stuck his head in my open bedroom doorway, bringing me from my thoughts. "We still on for chess this afternoon?"

I smiled. "Definitely."

"OK, see you then."

I cut my gaze to the clock on the nightstand, quickly closed my book, and jogged downstairs to the kitchen.

"Morning, Em," Domino greeted me with his usual smile.

I smiled back. "Good morning."

Aunt Tilly looked up from her coffee mug where she sat at the center island. "Hi, gorgeous, don't you look very put together this morning."

"Oh." I glanced down at the matching shorts and top my mom had bought for me and wished more than anything I could be wearing another one of my aunt's outfits. I grimaced internally. "Thanks," I sighed. "Mom bought them for me."

Aunt Tilly took a sip of her coffee. "Ya know, anytime you want to dive back into my closest, feel free."

I brought my eyes up to hers. "Really?"

She nodded. "Or . . . we could go shopping one afternoon at my favorite little place. What do you say?"

I smiled. "I think that sounds awesome." It sounded *more* than awesome.

Aunt Tilly gave me a sweet wink, and as I busied myself tying on my apron she dropped a kiss to my head on the way to her office.

My cell buzzed, snapping me to attention, and I checked the display. Grandmother. I hadn't talked to her since my arrival.

"Hello, Grandmother," I answered.

"Elizabeth Margaret, how are you?"

It felt very odd being called by my full name. "Fine, thank you."

"I had dinner with your parents last night and they knew I would be calling you this morning. They both say hello."

"That's nice." I'd forgotten how formal conversations were with her. This was almost painful! "Do you want to talk to Aunt Tilly?"

"No, I do not wish to talk to Matilda."

I wanted so much to tell my grandmother how great Tilly was, but I knew it would fall on deaf ears. Instead, I said, "You should talk to Frederick sometime. He's great."

Silence.

"So you are doing well?" she asked, ignoring my question. "Do you need anything? Money? More clothes? Anything?"

My lips curved into a sad smile. "I'm fine. Thank you, though. And Grandmother?"

"Yes?"

I took a deep breath. "Aunt Tilly told me . . . about Grandfather. I'm so sorry. I had no idea he died the day she was born."

I waited for a response, but only heard grandmother suck in a breath. "Grandmother?"

"Thank you for that."

"You're wel—"

"Now, your father," she interrupted, "asked me to remind you to keep up with your law reading. You don't want to start your internship already behind."

"OK," I answered, wishing that she would've said something about Grandfather instead.

"All right then. I'll call again next week. Good-bye, Elizabeth Margaret."

"Good-bye, Grandmo—"

She clicked off, and I stood there staring off into the kitchen at nothing in particular. I'd spent seventeen years with a person I felt about as comfortable with as a stranger. Yet I'd spent so little time at the Pepper House and felt more at home than I had in my whole life.

"Em, did you hear me?"

I glanced up at Domino. "Sorry. What'd you say?"

"I said you're in charge of the quiche this morning."

I paused, letting his words sink in. "I'm in charge of the . . . but that's the main dish."

He reached inside the refrigerator and pulled out a gallon of milk. "I know," he said, smiling.

I watched as he continued pulling out ingredients and then he tossed me a tomato. "See you in a bit." He closed the refrigerator and disappeared through the swinging doors.

"Domino?" I called after him. "Where are you going?"

"Get started," he yelled back.

Thirty minutes later he hadn't returned and I'd thrown myself into the project. I rolled out nine-inch crusts and lined multiple pie plates. I followed the recipe almost to a T, but added my secret ingredient of mustard to spice up the recipe.

On the crusts I spread Dijon and then layered it with mild deer sausage, tomatoes, green peppers, onions, and asiago-garlic shredded cheese. I whipped the eggs in equal parts yolks and whites, added milk, and carefully poured it down over the other ingredients.

Aunt Tilly, Frederick, and Beth came and went from the kitchen, but I barely noticed them as I immersed myself in the simple pleasure of putting together a delicious meal. And by the time I slipped the breakfast pies in the oven, I'd completely forgotten about my phone call with Grandmother.

In fact, I felt like a new person.

Domino finally reappeared. "OK, what do you want me to do?"

I gave him a disciplinary look, at which he innocently shrugged, and I laughed. "Let's get this fruit salad made."

Thirty minutes later the guests had been served, and Domino and I were in the process of cleaning the kitchen.

Aunt Tilly pushed through the swinging doors, carrying the first set of empty plates. I glanced up expectantly, eager to hear what the guests thought.

She looked right at me. "The couple in Cottage Two wants to know the recipe."

My eyes widened. "That's good, right?"

Aunt Tilly laughed. "That's more than good." She gave me a little shove. "Go on out and say hi."

I headed toward the door with a huge smile on my face. "A chef never tells her secret!"

Chapter Ten

A few days later, Domino and I had made a killer frittata for breakfast and were busy cleaning up.

"So, I don't know anything about you—and as your sous chef, I think I should know the basics."

Domino looked at me with raised eyebrows. "Um, OK."

"Where're you from?"

"Born and raised right here."

"Really?" I looked at him. "Somehow I pictured you vacationing here and never leaving."

Domino laughed. "I don't think I've ever been that free-spirited. I leave that kind of stuff to Tilly."

I took the plastic wrap and tore off a sheet. "I remember when I visited Brazil, Gwenny and I fantasized about just disappearing into the jungle and living our lives with one of the indigenous groups."

"Yep, that's definitely something your aunt would do." Domino laughed and handed me a bowl of sliced mango, and I spread the plastic wrap over it.

"I think Brazil is probably one of my favorite places." I put the mango in the refrigerator and closed the door. "Where's the coolest place you've been to?"

"Never been off the island."

"So, where'd you learn to cook?"

Domino squirted soap into a pan, took a scrubber, and started in. "Self-taught."

"Really? But you're so talented. I just assumed you'd been to culinary school."

He ran some water on the scrubber. "Why? You're self-taught."

I stopped with my wiping and stared at him for a second. He was right. I *was* self-taught.

"And you're pretty amazing," he added. "It's called talent. And we've both got it."

I kept standing there, just staring at him. I *did* have talent, I finally admitted to myself. Although I'd never thought of it that way before.

He went back to scrubbing the pan and I continued wiping things down.

"You any good at baking?" Domino asked me.

I crinkled my nose. "Other than a decent sugar cookie, desserts aren't really my thing."

"Me neither. Every chef's got their talent." He rinsed the pan. "Now, Beth's a good baker. She's always bringing in goodies she's made at home."

"Really?" I glanced around. "Where is she, by the way?"

Domino grabbed a towel and started drying the pan. "She's scrubbing grout today." He nodded toward the refrigerator. "She's probably thirsty."

"Oh, sure." I took my apron off, snatched a water bottle from the fridge, and went in search of Beth.

I headed out the back of the Pepper House and ran right into Cade. He wore the same red board shorts I'd already seen him in quite a few times, and once again, he had his shirt off. He crouched beside an old glider, tightening the screws. We still hadn't said much to each other since our disagreement over my mom and his dad.

I took a chance, hoping he was over it. "Hey," I greeted him.

He glanced up. "Hey," he said, and went right back to work.

I studied the sweaty, tanned muscles in his back as he continued tightening the screws. He turned a little and I caught another glimpse of the tiny ring he wore around his neck.

I searched for something friendly to say and remembered something my aunt had said. "Hey, Aunt Tilly said you surf?"

"Yep."

"I'd be up for a lesson if you're interested."

Cade glanced up at me again. He didn't say anything at first, just studied me. "Uh, OK, sure."

"Great." I smiled. "We friends again?"

He returned my smile with his sexy little half one that made me all mushy on the inside. "Friends."

"So, uh, maybe tomorrow?"

"Sure."

"Great." Cade smiled again.

I nodded to the cottage. "Beth in there?"

"Scrubbing grout."

I wrinkled my nose. "I heard."

"It's hard work."

I held up the water bottle. "Maybe this will help. See ya."

"Yeah, see ya."

I headed on toward the cottage, and as I neared it, I glanced back to Cade. He was looking at me, but quickly glanced away and went back to his work.

Smiling, I entered the cottage, to find Frederick and Beth down on their hands and knees scrubbing at the grout that separated the tiles. "Now, *that* looks fun."

They both glanced up at me with matching looks to kill.

I passed Beth the bottle of water, then wisely and quickly picked up a brush. "Need help?"

"Yes!" Frederick said.

I got down on my hands and knees to join them. If only my mom could see me now. She'd have a fit.

Two hours later we had scrubbed the entire cottage's tile floor, brushed on sealant, and kicked back with some cold sodas.

I popped the top on mine and looked across the cottage's kitchen at Beth. With the sleeve of her T-shirt, she wiped her face, and then stretched her neck from right to left. She looked absolutely exhausted.

"How long have you been here?" I asked.

She yawned. "Since six this morning. It takes about five

hours to do one cottage." She glanced at her watch. "I'll start in on the other one here in a few."

"Well, I don't have anything planned for the day. I'll help, and your five hours will be cut in half."

"Yeah, me, too," Frederick offered. "Scrubbing grout is definitely not a one-person job. This is crazy hard work."

"No!" Beth quickly argued. "That's ridiculous. You shouldn't have even helped me with this one. I'm getting paid for this. You're not."

Frederick shrugged. "What are friends for?"

By late that afternoon we were sufficiently sweaty and completely done with the other cottage. It was safe to say none of us wanted to see grout again for at least another year.

Beth threw everything into a bucket. "You two are incredible. Dinner. My treat."

Frederick and I didn't even hesitate. "Deal!"

"How 'bout the Crazy Chicken?" Beth asked. "They've got the best wings."

I smiled. "Sounds good."

"Meet you there in an hour." And with that she was gone. She rode her bike home to shower and change. Thirty minutes later Frederick and I were ready to go. We said bye to Aunt Tilly, found the van gone, and climbed onto one of the Pepper House's mopeds.

Frederick drove and I doubled behind him as he pulled out onto the coastal highway. Neither one of us spoke as we putt-putted along enjoying the warm breeze, the setting sun, and the expanse of ocean to our right.

Eventually we neared the marina. That huge boat still sat there floating at the end of the dock. I caught sight of a gray-haired gentleman sitting in the pilot house gazing out at the ocean. If he was a celebrity, I didn't recognize him.

"Do you know who owns that yacht?" I asked Frederick.

He glanced over his shoulder, studied the boat for a second, and shook his head. "No idea."

We lapsed back into silence as we continued along. Some time later he turned off to cut through the same cemetery Cade had shown me before. We peaked the hilltop and started down the other side, heading toward town.

In my peripheral vision I caught sight of a movement and turned to look. Sid stood in the distance with his head bowed as he stared at a grave. He glanced up at the same time and looked right at me.

I gave him a little wave and he nodded his head in return.

Minutes later we pulled into the small parking lot of the Crazy Chicken, where Beth stood waiting.

She smiled and waved. "Already got a table."

Frederick and I followed her through the crowded, outdoor restaurant and took a seat. People waved and yelled hellos to the three of us, reminding me once again what a small island it was. I was happy to be included in the hellos, even though I recognized only a few people.

We ordered virgin daiquiris, a bucket of wings, and a basket of fries. While Beth chatted with someone at the table beside us, I took a second to look around.

"Rustic" was the first word to pop into my head as I took

in the picnic-style tables, old-fashioned tools hanging from the rafters, and fans circling slowly overhead.

A waiter brought our daiquiris. "Hi," he said to me as he put the glass down.

"Hi," I replied, smiling into his too-cute dark eyes.

Beth turned away from her conversation. "Oh, good. I was hoping you'd stop by and say hi." She grabbed his arm. "Em, I want you to meet a good friend of mine, Jeremy. His parents own the place. Jeremy, this is Frederick's cousin, Em."

Jeremy and I shook hands.

"Nice to meet you. Welcome to the island. Are you here for the whole summer?" Jeremy asked.

"Just for the month," Beth answered for me. "She's staying at the Pepper. You two should get together."

I looked at her, wide-eyed. Could she be any more obvious?

Jeremy smiled. "Uh, yeah. That would be fun." He turned toward the kitchen. "Sorry, I gotta go. We're busy tonight."

I nodded. "Nice to meet you."

He wandered off, and I made no attempt to hide my interest. Tall, lanky, light-brown hair, tanned, clean-cut, great smile. Definitely my kind of guy.

Beth leaned in. "He's twenty and goes to college on the mainland. He's back for the summer. Super smart. Very nice. *And* single."

Super smart, nice, good-looking, *and* single. It didn't get much better than that. But there was something nagging at me, something I couldn't put my finger on.

"Perfect for a little summer romance," Beth suggestively teased.

I laughed. "You sound like my sister." But the idea definitely was intriguing. I pushed any nagging thoughts aside and mulled it over a bit as I sipped my drink.

Jeremy returned and put a stack of napkins in the center of our table. "Hey, how about tomorrow night?"

I didn't hide my surprise. "Sure!"

"Great! Can I have your cell number?"

I wrote it down on a napkin and handed it to him.

"I'll give you a call." With a warm smile for me, he headed off.

"See." Beth sashayed her shoulders. "Now you're all set."

I smiled. I couldn't believe it was that easy!

* * *

Just like he said, the next morning Jeremy called. "I've only got a few minutes. I'm opening the restaurant this morning. But how about I pick you up at six tonight? We'll do dinner?"

"Sounds great."

"OK, see you then. I'm looking forward to it."

"Me too." I grinned as I hung up. I couldn't believe I had a date. Gwenny would be shocked! I quickly texted her and headed downstairs, where I ran into Aunt Tilly.

"Good morning," I singsonged. "I've got a date tonight," I told her all in one breath.

She whirled away from where she stood studying the bookshelf. "Good morning to you, too. And a date?" She gave a little excited hop. "Ooh, with who?"

I smiled at her silliness. "Jeremy. His parents—"

"Own the Crazy Chicken. Oh, he's so nice. He's from a good family. And he's handsome."

I laughed.

Grinning, she clapped her hands with an excited thought. "Now we definitely have to go shopping!"

"Shopping?"

"Yes, for clothes. A new outfit. Doesn't that sound like fun?"

Actually, I couldn't think of anything better. "I'd love to! But I'm supposed to go surfing with Cade. Let me just tell him I'm heading off with you."

"Oh, well, I don't want to mess up your plans with Cade."

I waved her off. "No, I want to go with you. I'm sure Cade won't mind."

I found him in the side yard pruning the bushes. "Hi."

He smiled up at me and it shot warmth straight through my body.

"Aunt Tilly wants to take me shopping. Can we surf tomorrow?"

His smile dropped a little and I immediately felt horrible. "I'm sorry to cancel last-minute."

"No, it's OK. Surf's not that good today anyway. We'll try same time tomorrow." He went back to the bushes. "Have fun with Tilly."

"Thanks." I took a few steps away and glanced back to Cade. He seemed so focused on clipping the bush. I hoped he wasn't too upset.

Within minutes Aunt Tilly had left Domino and Frederick

in charge of things, grabbed our bags, and we were heading into town for a day of shopping.

I couldn't remember ever being so excited about going shopping. My mom and I never did anything so spontaneous. "This is going to be fun."

"This is going to be beyond fun. You'll love this place I'm taking you to."

Aunt Tilly turned on some '70s rock music. "Em?"

"Hm?"

"You being here means the world to me."

We shared a smile. "Thanks, Aunt Tilly."

She slipped on her sunglasses and started singing to the music. Minutes later, we pulled into a small store with retro flowers painted all over it. We got out and Aunt Tilly linked fingers with me as we strolled inside. Air-conditioning, mild vanilla incense, wonderful clothes, and an old lady in a smart business suit and chic short gray hair greeted us.

"Tilly!" The old lady waved and looked right at me. "And you've *got* to be Em."

I smiled. "Yes, ma'am."

Tilly put her arm around me. "Em, this is Grammy."

"Grammy?"

The older woman let out a husky laugh. "Everyone on this island calls me Grammy. Now, what can I do for you?" she asked.

"Em needs some new clothes," Aunt Tilly volunteered. "She likes my style, but needs her own twist."

With a deep inhalation through her nostrils, Grammy steepled her fingers against her pursed lips and studied me.

She twirled her finger in the air, indicating I should turn, and I obeyed, rotating in a slow circle.

When I came back around, Grammy clapped her hands. "Got it."

And then she was off. Like a tornado whipping through the store, she pulled things off the racks and started stacking them in a dressing room.

My eyes wandered to a painting hanging behind the checkout counter. It was of a dad and son fishing. I recognized the same realistic style and colors as the others I'd admired. But this one felt sadder.

Aunt Tilly tugged my arm and my attention away from the painting and led me to a couple of wicker seats. "Let her have free rein," she whispered. "She knows her clothes and people. You'll see."

I watched, my excitement building, trying to keep track of what all she was pulling off racks. After about a dozen or so outfits, it occurred to me. "Aunt Tilly, I've only got about two hundred dollars."

And if my mom found out I'd spent it on these clothes, I silently added, she would *not* be happy.

Aunt Tilly fluttered her fingers. "My treat."

"No," I whispered. "You can't do that."

She looked at me. "Listen, you've been helping out around the B&B since you got here and you've got a couple of weeks to go yet. Consider this your paycheck." She winked at me. "No argument."

A couple of weeks to go yet. That thought brought a contented sigh. Plenty of time to enjoy this awesome new

place. Plenty of time before I had to go back . . . *go back* . . .
Slowly my contentment became melancholy as I thought of the
rigid environment back home.

I glanced over at my aunt and studied her pretty profile as
she watched Grammy. My thoughts began circling around her,
my mom, my grandmother, and whatever family feud there
was between them. If anyone was going to tell me what it was,
it would probably be my free-spirited aunt.

With that thought I took a deep breath and boldly asked,
"Aunt Tilly, what is going on with you and my mom and
grandmother? It can't be all about Grandfather's death."

She looked down, a frown slowly curving her lips, and
sighed. "No, it's not about your grandfather's death. There's
just a lot of . . . history. Your grandmother and I, we're very
different."

"But Gwenny and I didn't even know you existed until you
sent that graduation card."

"I know." Aunt Tilly smoothed her hand over my head.
"There's a lot to explain there. Too much to talk about here.
The past is the past. I've moved on. I know your mom and
grandmother have too."

"But you and Mom used to be so close. What happened?"
Tilly sighed.

"OK!" Grammy excitedly announced, interrupting us.
"Time to start trying on."

"But I didn't even tell you my size," I protested. Or the fact
I sometimes have to buy petite because I'm so short. Or the
fact—

Grammy laughed. "Dear, I've done this my whole life. I know your size better than you do."

Aunt Tilly gave me a nudge, and, reluctantly ending the conversation, I disappeared into the dressing room. Grammy was right. She *did* know my size. And my style. And my colors. And my everything.

I tried on outfit after outfit, absolutely loving it all. Grammy had done a perfect job of giving me that flowy, casual look but with my own twist.

A smocked top with leggings. A silvery knee-length sundress. Drawstring capris with a striped tank top. The list went on and on.

Everything managed to make me look slender and taller. It was a miracle, and I felt absolutely great about myself.

Realizing it was getting late, I decided to keep a cute polo mini dress on. Aunt Tilly and I paid Grammy and loaded up the van. We got home in just enough time for me to dump my bags, freshen up, and hightail it outside to wait for Jeremy.

As I stood there in the late-afternoon sun waiting on my date, I found myself feeling more confident than ever. I looked great. I felt great. I *was* great.

JUST WENT SHOPPING! I texted Gwenny. U SHLD SEE ALL MY COOL CLOTHES. MOM WLD NOT APPROVE.

WHO CARES?

I laughed at that. And out of the corner of my eye, I caught sight of someone coming around the side of the Pepper House. I didn't have to fully look to know it was Cade.

"Well, hey, you look nice."

"Thanks."

"Have fun with Tilly?"

"I did. We bought the store out."

He laughed and looked me up and down before glancing around. "You waiting on somebody?"

"Jeremy," I quickly answered, suddenly feeling very awkward.

"Oh." He studied me a second. "You guys going on a date or something?"

I nodded, my awkwardness increasing tenfold, and started fiddling with my purse. "Um, well, sort of."

"He's a . . . he's a nice guy. Seems like your type, I guess."

I looked up questioningly. My type? What did that mean? And did I detect a note of regret in Cade's voice?

We both stood there, saying nothing.

Jeremy pulled in then, giving a little honk. I turned away from Cade and gave Jeremy a smile and a wave. "Well, see ya later," I said to Cade, and climbed into Jeremy's car.

"Yeah, later," I heard him mumble.

Jeremy pulled away and I glanced in my side mirror. Cade still stood there, watching us drive away.

I kept my eyes on him all the way down the drive until Jeremy rounded the corner and Cade left my sight. I couldn't help wondering what Cade was thinking.

Chapter Eleven

*J*eremy was the kind of guy my parents would have loved.

He was the epitome of perfection.

He opened doors for me.

He complimented me on how nice I looked.

He asked me lots of questions about myself.

He was cute, smart, witty.

He was perfect—too perfect—too much like my parents and my life back in New England. Which was probably why I could do nothing but think about Cade.

Smiling, I nodded at Jeremy's comment regarding the Republican Party. I didn't really have a strong opinion about politics.

I took a nibble of my bland grilled fish. If someone, *anyone*, in the kitchen would've ground sea salt and malabar pepper, and squeezed some lemon on this fish, it would've been greatly improved. Salt, pepper, and lemon. Not too much to ask of folks.

"Anyway," Jeremy said with a sigh, "growing up here wasn't so bad. But I'm definitely glad to be away at college. Of course, to you first-timers, this place is paradise."

I nudged my plate away and propped my knife and fork on the side. What a shame; that had been a perfectly good piece of sea bass.

My brain got back on track, quickly recalling what Jeremy had just said. "Yes, this place is paradise." It was too bad he didn't realize that.

Cade seemed to appreciate it, and he was from here too.

What am I doing thinking about Cade while I'm on a date with Jeremy?

I cleared my throat. "How long have your parents owned the Crazy Chicken?"

"Since before I was born. My grandparents owned it before them."

"Wow, your family really does go back a long way."

He smiled at that.

Our dessert came and we ate it in a mostly comfortable silence. It was almost like we were an old married couple. Finally it was time for the bill.

We left the restaurant and Jeremy drove me home. We talked about travel—all the places we'd seen and the cities we wanted to visit. Jeremy and I had a lot of things in common. I really couldn't think of a better, more perfect first date. Except that I couldn't get the image out of my brain of Cade standing and watching as we pulled away.

Jeremy stopped in front of the Pepper House, got out, and came around to open my door. My stomach fluttered a little bit with the expectation of a kiss good night.

Gently, Jeremy took my hand. "I really had a nice time. Thanks for the date."

I smiled. "Thanks. Me too."

He lowered his head and pressed his lips to mine. I returned the kiss, expecting . . . I don't know, excitement, passion. But it was only a quick kiss, and after he pulled away, he placed a sweet peck on my cheek. "Meeting you has definitely brightened up my summer. I'll call you tomorrow."

I smiled, willing myself to be excited for his phone call tomorrow.

Jeremy gave my hand an affectionate squeeze before getting in his car and pulling away.

I stood there watching his taillights, replaying the kiss in my head. It'd been a nice, proper, first kiss. *A nice, proper, first kiss?* Who was I, my mom?

Gwenny would want to know if it'd been hot. *Did it wow you?* I could hear her asking.

No, it hadn't wowed me. It'd been sweet. There was nothing wrong with sweet. Sweet was good. Right?

"So are you two official?"

With a start, I swung around. Cade stood in the shadows of the Pepper House.

"You scared me to death. What are you doing here?"

"There was a plumbing leak in Cottage Two, and your aunt called me. I was just on my way home and saw you two pull in."

And he'd just stood there and watched us kiss? My face grew warm in embarrassment. "You should have coughed or something to let us know you were there."

"Sorry." He emerged from the shadows and I swallowed the sudden nervousness in my throat. The tilt of his smiling lips drew my attention, and it seemed all I could stare at as he came closer.

I tried to think of something to say, but for the life of me I couldn't even remember what he'd just said.

He came to a stop in front of me. My mind screamed for me to do something, say something, but all I managed was to continue standing there, staring at his lips.

Cade shifted ever so slightly and his soapy scent filled my senses. "Good night, Em," he whispered, and then disappeared into the night.

I stayed right where I was, staring at nothing in particular, listening to my rapid breaths, feeling my heart bang against my chest wall. It was what I had expected earlier, with Jeremy, but Cade hadn't even kissed me.

Eventually, I managed a swallow.

My cell buzzed and I jumped about a mile into the air. "Hello?" I answered, slightly out of breath.

"Well," Gwenny greeted me. "You sound winded. Did I interrupt you and Jeremy making out?"

I laughed. "No."

"Sooo, tell me about the date."

As I walked up to my room, I told her about the dinner, the friendliness, the good-night kiss. "But . . ."

"But?" she prompted.

"It was all fine. But then Cade was here when I got home, and he saw the good-night kiss, and I don't know, he was right in front of me and I could barely breathe, and—"

"What did he do?"

I sighed. "Nothing. He told me good night, whispered it actually."

"Whispered it?"

"Oh, Gwenny, he smelled so good. And he wasn't even touching me and I could feel his warmth, he was standing that close."

"Em," my sister sighed, "he sounds amazing. They both do actually. I think I'm jealous."

"Don't be. I'm completely confused right now."

"Go out with both of them."

"Gwenny, that's not me. You know that." I paused. "You know what else?"

"What?"

"I'm going surfing with Cade tomorrow."

"Good, you can get to know him better. And you can wear your new bikini! See, it's really perfect!"

"I don't know. I think it's just going to be awkward."

"You'll be fine. Just act like nothing happened, have fun, and look hot in your bikini. That's it!"

"Sure. It's just that easy." I sighed, suddenly not looking forward to tomorrow. "OK, I'll call you and let you know how it went."

"Great! And Em, seriously, just relax have fun."

I hung up the phone. I would try, but I knew already that I'd be distracted . . . by Cade.

* * *

Breakfast came and went, but I barely remembered scrambling the eggs, as preoccupied with my surfing lesson as I was.

Cade stopped into the kitchen as Domino and I were cleaning up. "We still on for surfing?"

I smiled. "Definitely!"

"Thirty minutes?"

"I'll be there."

I peeked my head into Frederick's room. "What should I wear for surfing?"

He looked up from his laptop. "What have you got?"

"Two bikinis."

He went over to his dresser and pulled out a shirt. "This is a rash guard. Throw this on over your top and you should be good to go."

I took the shirt from him. "Cool, thanks."

I put on my blue-and-white bikini, not the one Gwenny bought me. I knew she'd be mad I wasn't looking "hot," but I needed to focus. I met Cade out front of the Pepper House.

"Hey, don't you look all surfer girl."

I motioned to my outfit. "Rash guard, courtesy of Frederick."

He'd secured a surfboard to a bracket off the side of the moped. "Climb on," he said, and did the same.

"Oh, we're not taking the van?"

"Nope."

"Uh, OK." I swung my leg over and sat behind him while he turned the key.

"We're going to Parquito Bay," he told me. "It's got good beginner waves."

Cade rolled the moped forward and puttered off down the driveway. He turned onto the coastal highway and picked up speed. I looked for a place to put my hands and finally decided to hold on to his waist.

He scooted back on the seat, getting comfortable, putting our bodies even closer. I could feel his ripped abs under his soft T-shirt. His soapy scent swirled around me, and I leaned forward a little to inhale.

About fifteen minutes later he pulled off to the side of the road and cut the engine. "We're here. Go on down." He started unhooking the board from the bracket. "I'll be there in a sec with the board."

I swung my leg over and walked between the sand dunes onto Parquito Beach. I flung my flip-flops to the side and headed down to the water's edge. Sunlight sent dancing beams across the turquoise water as it rolled to shore, and I wondered how a place could be so beautiful.

"What do you think?" Cade asked, coming up beside me.

"It's absolutely gorgeous. How is it possible for a place to be so perfect?"

He gazed out over the water. "I know. I can't imagine ever leaving."

I glanced over at him. "Really?"

Cade shrugged. "This is home. I love it here."

The matter-of-factness in his voice made me smile. "I can see why." I thought of Jeremy then and how he'd said just the opposite. He couldn't wait to get out off the island. It was as though he couldn't appreciate what he had.

"So, looks like we've got the beach to ourselves. Good thing. You won't hit anybody then."

"Hey!" I defended myself, although I knew he had a point.

Cade laughed and nodded to the surfboard behind us. "I already waxed it, so we're good to go."

He slipped off his T-shirt and tossed it up the beach. I took in a delicious second of his tanned chest before he lay down on the board.

"This is a long board. It's good for small waves. Good learner board. So, what we're going to practice first is just getting up on your knees." From his lying-down position, he mimicked paddling with his arms, then he lifted up and swung his knees under him, landing about center on the board. "Now you try."

He moved out of the way and I stretched out belly-down on the board, hoping beyond hope that my bikini-clad butt looked good. I paddled, lifted up, and brought my knees under, easily mimicking Cade. He reached down and repositioned my left knee, and I caught my breath at his closeness.

"Try to keep one knee in front for stability."

I nodded.

"All right, now let's try feet." We switched positions, him on the board and me watching. Holding on to the sides, he jumped to his feet. "I surf left. You'll just have to see what feels right to you."

He moved and I practiced jumping to my feet, feeling pretty confident, but wishing he'd make another adjustment to my knees or something.

"Looks good," he complimented. "Now, let's get in the water."

Taking the board, Cade and I waded into the ocean, diving through the waves as we got farther out. He stopped when the water hit us chest-high. With his hand on the board, he smiled across at me with pure happiness in his blue eyes. "Ready?"

"Definitely."

"OK, get on up, and I'll push you into the right wave. When you feel it lift you, that's when you try to get to your knees."

I nodded as a wave rolled past us, sending us both up and down with the swell. I hopped onto the board and toppled right over the other side—straight into Cade.

He grabbed for me as I went under, and when I surfaced a wave pushed me into him. He held me tight against him, laughing.

I swallowed, trying to play it cool. I wiped the water from my eyes and moved my hair out of my face. "Glad to provide you with some morning entertainment," I deadpanned, thoroughly mortified but trying not to show it.

He repositioned our bodies, wrapping his arm around my waist, and I nearly stopped breathing.

"Let's try this again," he said, and effortlessly swung me up onto the board. He looked toward the ocean and the waves.

"Ready . . . ready . . . ready . . . OK *now*! Paddle!"

He pushed me forward, and I paddled with my arms. The wave lifted me, I grabbed onto the board, brought my knees up under me, and before I knew it, I was surfing! "Yeeeaaah!!!" I shouted.

I rode the wave all the way to shore until the board bottomed out on sand and I fell off. I whipped around and found Cade in the water pumping the air with both his fists.

"Awesome!" he yelled as he swam toward me. He came up right beside me, grabbed me up in a huge hug, and swung me around. "That was great for a first time," he said.

As he put me down on the sand I looked up at him, grinning. He looked down at me and suddenly everything stopped. I looked in his eyes as he leaned into me and then I felt his lips on mine.

Gwenny always talked about a "wow factor," and I instantly felt that. I leaned into him as he deepened the kiss, feeling the whole world fall away, like we were the only two people existing.

He pulled away, looking a little lost and uncomfortable. "Uh, OK, let's get back in the water," he said, and he scooped up the board and headed back into the ocean.

I stood on the beach, not really knowing what just happened, unable to move for a few seconds. Finally, I shook my head to clear my haze and followed Cade. My thoughts were going to have to wait. I just needed to focus on surfing— not on Cade, his amazing kiss, or how different he and Jeremy were. I'd deal with that later.

Now it was time to surf.

* * *

Later that day, after Cade dropped me off back at the Pepper House, I found myself in the kitchen. I had left a message for Gwenny, begging her to call me back as soon as humanly possible. All I could think about was the kiss. I still couldn't believe it happened, and how totally amazing it was, almost the complete opposite of Jeremy's sweet, "proper" first-date kiss. Cade's was just . . . wow.

"So, you almost ready?" Domino said, interrupting my thoughts. He nodded to the dish I was plating. As he had asked, I prepared the entire brunch meal for him for his approval.

"Yup, just another minute."

He nodded and walked back to the dining room. I finished cleaning off the edges of the plate and, with nerves jostling my stomach, I carried it into the dining room, where Domino waited.

"Pecan-crusted salmon," I told him, "with raspberry sauce. Jasmine rice with dried fruit. Garlic roasted asparagus. And mango mousse for dessert."

"Ooh, that sounds delicious!" Domino said a napkin over his lap. "I have been looking so forward to this."

I put the plate down in front of him, and, with a deep breath, took a step back.

"Now, don't be nervous," he told me, forking off a flaky chunk of the salmon.

I watched as he put it into his mouth.

He tried some rice next, then asparagus. No emotion showed on his face, which added to my anxiety.

Domino paused, then put his fork down, wiped his mouth with the napkin, and placed it beside his plate.

I took one look at his face and knew. "You don't like it."

He gave me a tender smile. "Well." He paused again, taking a deep breath. "Sweetie, please don't be upset. I've messed up recipes before. Especially when I'm trying to be creative."

My heart dropped. "Messed up?"

"Honey, the salmon would be better if it was almond-crusted, not pecan. The sauce should be strawberry, not raspberry. And the asparagus should be parmesan, not garlic. I appreciate what you're trying to do, but it's not really working."

"Oh." I tried not to get upset, but I'd never had anyone criticize my cooking before. I should have known all of this too. I was mad at myself, getting so caught up in Cade's kiss, not focusing on my cooking.

Domino motioned for me to sit down, and I did, though reluctantly.

"Em, I know you're going to realize this once you think about it. Right now you're upset."

"I'm not upset," I corrected him, although I really was.

Domino nodded. "You have to think about complementary tastes. Strawberry, almonds, and salmon? Parmesan asparagus with a bite of jasmine rice? Pecans and raspberries are great in muffins, but with a pink fish?"

I sighed, absorbing what he was saying, comprehending in my mind he had a point. He *did* know what he was doing. But at the same time I was *really* disappointed. I wanted to wow him with a twist on the recipes.

He sat quietly, watching me take it all in. Watching me mull it all over in my head.

"Does this mean I don't get to make the featured meal?"

Domino tilted his head to the side. "Of course you're still cooking. But I do need you to make adjustments. It is my kitchen," he gently reminded me. "When it's your kitchen you'll get to call the shots."

He reached over and squeezed my hand. "Now, tuck in your bottom lip and go make those changes to the shopping list."

I smiled. "Thanks, Domino."

"And you know I'm going to be looking over your shoulder the whole time you're preparing it," he playfully warned me.

I laughed. "I have no doubt."

* * *

The next morning I threw my covers aside and got out of bed. It was farmers' market day. The next day was brunch day. I was glad I had something to occupy my mind after the surfing lesson with Cade. I hadn't seen him much at all since then, which was fine. What wasn't fine was that Gwenny hadn't called me back, and I was dying to talk to her about what had happened.

I got myself ready and headed downstairs.

"Good morning, gorgeous!" Aunt Tilly greeted me with her usual enthusiasm.

"Good morning." I turned to Domino. "Did you see my revised shopping list?"

He smiled. "Looks good," he said, and nodded to a giant cooler sitting next to the table. "That's for the farmers' market. Have fun."

"Let me go get my bag," I said, and trotted up the back steps.

"Get your bathing suit too," Aunt Tilly called after me, "we're dropping the food back here then heading straight to the beach."

I ran into my room, quickly threw my suit on, and redressed, got my purse, snatched my beach bag from the closet, and hightailed it back downstairs.

Aunt Tilly and Beth were waiting in the van with the engine running. I slid open the side door and jumped in.

"Farmers' market and the beach," Beth told me. "It's going to be a total girls' day!"

I smiled, glad that Beth was coming along. A girls' day was exactly what I needed!

"So, what's on the menu?" Beth asked as Tilly pulled away from the Pepper House.

"Well, of course the usual brunchy eggs, bacon, pancakes, et cetera. But my part of the whole thing will be almond-crusted salmon with strawberry sauce," I said, quoting the revised menu. "Jasmine rice with dried fruit. Parmesan-roasted asparagus. And mango mousse for dessert."

Beth looked over her shoulder at me. "Yum."

I smiled. "I'm going for a fruity, island theme."

Aunt Tilly headed down the coastal highway. "It's going to be great. We're going to have a full house, too. We've got a family of four checking into Cottage One later today. I told them all about our famous Sunday brunch and they're very excited. It'll be a great start to their vacation."

I couldn't wait to tell Gwenny all about it.

We drove along the coastal highway until we reached the marina where Sid's boat had been docked. Where there had been a nearly empty parking lot before, tiny booths now jammed the area. Big umbrellas shaded the booths from the island sun. Lots of cars, trucks, and mopeds were wedged into any available spots and tons of people milled about.

Aunt Tilly pulled in behind a rusted-out car and cut the engine.

"Looks like the whole island's here," I commented, sliding open the side door.

"Oh this is nothing." Beth jumped out of the passenger side. "You should come sometime at dawn."

I grabbed my bag and the grocery list and slid the side door closed. "How often is this here?"

"Every Saturday," my aunt answered, leading the way. "Usually Domino comes and does the shopping for the Pepper House."

As we wove our way through the parked cars, I glanced down at the water toward Sid's boat and saw that he was gone. For Cade's sake, I guessed that was good.

Aunt Tilly waved at someone who yelled hello. "Whatever you buy, just tell them to deliver it to the van. Cooler's in the back. They know what to do. They'll send us a bill."

I nodded and began strolling through the booths, surveying

the amazingly eclectic selection, from fresh seafood to herbs to olives to artisan cheese. Everything was organic and homemade. It was culinary bliss for me, and I wanted to buy something from each booth.

"Hi," I greeted a boy sitting on a stool behind an oversized cooler. A note stuck to the top of the cooler read ATLANTIC SALMON.

He gave a nod, his mannerisms looking much older than he appeared. "All fresh."

I smiled. "I'm sure. Ten pounds, please."

His eyes lit up. "Great!"

I laughed a little at that. "Just deliver it to the Pepper House's van."

I continued on my way, talking to vendors here and there, and placing more orders off my list.

"You look like you're in heaven."

I glanced up to see Jeremy standing beside me and smiled. "Hey, there!" I said. It was nice to see him. But my thoughts flashed to Cade and our surfing lesson. I shook my head and refocused on Jeremy. "I am. This is like a dream come true." I'd have to talk Domino into letting me come with him next Saturday, too.

Jeremy picked up a mango and lightly squeezed it. "Word around town is Domino's letting you make Sunday brunch."

"Word around town is correct." I picked up a mango too, and tried it for ripeness.

"Suppose there's enough room for me to come?" Jeremy asked.

I put that mango aside and tried another. "Oh, sure, I don't think Aunt Tilly would mind." Plus, I'd planned for a few extra people just in case.

"OK, good. See you tomorrow, then." And with a quick kiss on my cheek, he was gone.

Aunt Tilly came up beside me. "Cade says hi."

I looked around, my stomach jittering a bit. "Cade's here?"

"He's here every Saturday. His friend runs a juice stand and he helps out." Tilly held up a glass of carrot juice and nodded across the way.

I glanced over to a booth lined with palm fronds where Cade was currently waiting on a girl about my age. He chuckled at something she said and handed her a glass with red juice. I wondered if he'd seen me with Jeremy.

"That looks good." I motioned to the carrot juice. "I'm going to go get some."

"You done shopping?" Aunt Tilly asked.

I nodded.

"Couple minutes then, and we're heading off."

Cade caught sight of me walking toward him and gave me a half smile. He didn't look away as I sidestepped a couple of kids and approached the juice booth.

"Hey," he greeted me, studying my face. "You're sunburned."

I crinkled my red nose. "And about to be more. Aunt Tilly and Beth and I are heading to the beach." I glanced at the juice menu. "I'll have a carrot and ginger, please."

"My favorite." He turned and grabbed a few carrots from the ice bin. "Which beach?"

I shrugged. "No idea."

Cade fed a couple of carrots into the juice machine. He cut a sliver of ginger off a fresh root and sent it through the juicer too. "So big day tomorrow with the brunch and all."

"Yep. Um, are you going to be there?"

Cade handed me a plastic glass with the foamy juice. "Wouldn't miss it."

I smiled and took a sip.

"On the house for my surfer girl."

"Thanks," I said, staring into his eyes.

"So, about yester—" he started, but Beth bounded up beside me.

"Hey. You about ready?"

"Uh, sure," I said, looking back at Cade. What I really wanted to do was stay right here with him. I wanted to talk about yesterday, see what he was thinking.

Cade didn't take his eyes off of me. "Have fun. I'll see you tomorrow."

I nodded and waved as Beth dragged me away to the van. I walked after her, but when I looked back, Cade was still staring at me.

Chapter Twelve

Aunt Tilly, Beth, and I zipped home, dropped off the food, and headed straight to the beach. When we arrived, we pulled off the side of the road, parked under a huge palm tree, and piled out.

I followed them down a narrow sand path, bordered on both sides by high dunes, onto a secluded beach that looked like something straight out of a magazine.

Off-white sand covered the area, its powdery texture devoid of shells. Roughly twenty feet farther on lapped a calm, vibrant ocean that stretched all the way to the horizon. I glanced around, discovering we were in a small inlet with a beach bordered by sand dunes and huge boulders. I estimated the entire place to be about half the size of a football field.

Off to the far left lay the only people on the beach. And

from the distance I stood, squinting in the sun, I honestly couldn't tell if the couple were women or men or one of each.

Beth dropped her towel and yanked off her shirt and shorts to reveal a turquoise bikini, then sprinted into the water. A few seconds later, her giggle floated back to us.

"She does that every time we come," Aunt Tilly said.

I smiled at her comment, but found myself oddly envious that my aunt and Beth had such a great relationship. That Beth had had more time with my aunt than I had. That she'd known her longer.

"Come on." Aunt Tilly picked up Beth's stuff and led me all the way over to the right. "There's hardly anybody here. For a Saturday, I expected it to be much more packed."

Aunt Tilly busied herself laying out our towels. "We locals like to keep this place quiet. The tourists have tons of other beaches they can make use of."

I liked the fact I was now in the elite "locals" category.

In my peripheral vision I caught sight of a huge yacht circling in the distance around the island. I studied it a second, recognizing it as the one from the marina.

I took off my T-shirt and shorts.

"Great suit," Tilly said, nodding at my black-and-gold bikini.

"Thanks. Gwenny bought it for me. I wasn't even sure if I'd be brave enough to wear it. It's kinda stringy."

Aunt Tilly smiled. "You can totally pull it off."

As she closed her eyes and soaked in the sun, I sat for a moment taking in the scenery.

"So, how was your date with Jeremy?" Aunt Tilly asked a few minutes later.

I lay back on my towel and closed my eyes. "It was fine. He's nice. He's coming for brunch tomorrow. I hope that's OK?"

"Sure." She shifted, nestling herself into the towel and sand. "But 'fine' and 'nice'? Not really zing-zang-zoom words?"

"Zing-zang-zoom?"

"Yeah, you know, does he 'rock your world'?"

I laughed at that. "I don't know. He's sweet. We've had only one date. It takes more than that to figure out the 'rock-your-world' part, right?"

Although one tiny whisper and an unexpected kiss from Cade had most certainly "rocked my world."

"Yeah, give it some time. You never know what might spark."

"You sound like you're speaking from experience."

Aunt Tilly didn't answer for a few seconds. I turned my head to look at her profile as she continued lying there, baking in the sun.

She must have felt my stare because she opened her left eye and looked right back at me.

I smiled a little.

"Frederick's dad," she answered softly.

My interest piqued at her quiet admission and the emotion ringing strong and true in her voice.

"Will you tell me about him? Was he why you came down here, away from Mom and Grandmother?"

She continued staring at me for quite a while, and the more she stared, the harder my heart beat. I wanted so bad to know her secrets and what had made her into the incredible person she was today.

"Sorry, was that too forward?"

With a sigh, Aunt Tilly turned back to soaking in the sun. "No, no. It's fine. I never did like living in your grandmother's house. Too many rules. Too much properness. Too much everything. I was always rebellious, sneaking out, purposefully doing things to make her angry. I look back on that now and am certainly not proud of my behavior. When I was sixteen, I got in trouble. Your grandmother helped me out, with one condition. That I leave and never come back."

"What?" I gasped. "She kicked you out?"

Aunt Tilly nodded. "And so I left," she continued. "I came here and got a job cleaning the Pepper House. The owner, Roger Pepper, was much older and very handsome. He made no secret of his interest in me, but I continually turned him down. Time wore on and I softened. We became romantic and soon Frederick came about. When Frederick was just a small boy, Roger died and left the Pepper to me." She took a deep breath. "And here I am."

"Wow," I said, taking in the story. I was realizing more and more what an amazing woman Tilly was. And my grandmother . . . I didn't even know what to think about her anymore.

"Mm," she halfheartedly agreed.

"But what did you do that was so serious to get you kicked out of Grandmother's house?"

Aunt Tilly sighed and got up. "That's for some other time," she answered, and strolled down to the water. "By the way," she called back to me, "this is a topless beach if you feel like it." With that, she untied her top and slung it aside.

"Wait, what?!" A topless beach? I watched as she joined Beth swimming out into the bay.

How different this place was from my life back home. How different Tilly was. No wonder she felt stifled by our family.

With a sigh I closed my eyes. My brain swirled with Tilly's story and the teenager she'd been. What could have gotten her kicked out? I wondered. A serious crime? Somehow I couldn't picture my aunt actually committing a felony.

I snuggled farther into my towel and thought about Roger Pepper. What kind of person was he to have captured such a free spirit as my aunt? He must have been an incredible person for sure. A patient one, too. I imagined it took a lot of that to handle my aunt's independence.

So if her story held true, that she slowly fell in love with a man where there had originally been no zing, then possibly Jeremy could be the love of my life . . . ? But then what about Cade?

Inside my beach bag, I heard my phone buzzing. I reached in, saw it was my sister, and hit the Call button. "You will never believe this, but I'm on a topless beach," I told Gwenny, laughing.

"*You're where?!*"

I shot straight up. "Mom?"

Chapter Thirteen

I lay awake the next morning bogged down with guilt, cringing just thinking about the damage control I had to do. What was my mom doing using my sister's phone, anyway? And why did I have to go and be stupid? With my uncharacteristically big mouth I just had to announce to my mother that I was on a topless beach.

Thank God I hadn't actually been topless—or joked that I was. My mother probably would've chartered a private plane to come get me personally if I had.

But I was still in trouble. My aunt was in trouble. Mom was threatening to make me come home. Everything was a mess.

My mom had insisted on speaking to Matilda immediately. And so I'd hurried down to the ocean's edge. I waved the phone in the air and yelled for Aunt Tilly.

With the phone muted, I explained to her what had happened, and offered up a quick apology. She'd taken the phone from me. I could hear my mom's angry voice filtering through the speaker, and I couldn't help it, I started to cry.

We'd left the beach immediately and driven home in silence, dropping Beth off on the way. I had wanted to say something to Aunt Tilly, but I didn't know what.

There I lay in my bed, watching the ceiling fan slowly whirl, a million apologies on my tongue, knowing I would be packing my bags to go home. I couldn't begin to think about what I'd miss here—my newfound family, my freedom, Jeremy, and . . . Cade. I'd have to say good-bye to all of it, and I wasn't sure I could.

All on the day I was supposed to make my Sunday brunch.

I sighed as someone knocked on my door. "Come in," I said, sitting up.

Aunt Tilly opened my door and stuck her head in. "Is the coast clear? No screaming mothers on the phone?"

I huffed out a laugh mixed with a relieved cry. "You're not angry with me?"

"Oh, honey." Tilly closed my door and came the rest of the way in. "Never." She sat down on my bed and pulled me into her arms.

Tears pressed my eyes and I gave into them as she held me. "I'm so sorry."

"You didn't do anything wrong."

I sniffed. "I shouldn't have said anything. Mom yelled at you. I got you in trouble."

Aunt Tilly rubbed my back. "Oh, please. *You* did not get me in trouble. *I've* been in trouble with my family for as long as I can remember."

I let out a watery laugh.

Aunt Tilly released our hug, cradled my face in her hands in a motherly sort of way, and gave me the most tender, loving look.

I sniffed. "Am I going home?"

Gently, Tilly rubbed her thumbs over my wet cheeks. "You're not going home until you decide to go home. I spoke with your mom again last night after she'd calmed down. And I spoke to your grandmother as well." She smiled. "Everything's OK. Just next time promise me you won't trust your caller ID?"

I smiled and nodded. "I promise."

"Now, I've got a Sunday brunch waiting for you to make it. Get cleaned up and get downstairs. Domino's waiting."

Aunt Tilly left and I climbed out of bed. I wouldn't say I felt like a weight had been lifted, but I definitely felt better than I had when I woke up.

I got myself together and headed downstairs. I had a brunch to prepare. Twenty minutes later I was peeling the bottom half inch of the asparagus and Domino was adding olive oil to the almonds and bread-crumb mixture.

Just as I was getting into a groove, my cell buzzed, and I checked the display. Gwenny—I hoped. I answered the phone hoping it wasn't my mother. "Hello?"

"Oh my God, I can't believe you sunbathed topless!" Gwenny screamed.

"Next time you lend Mom your phone," I told Gwenny, "can you please text me with a warning?"

Gwenny laughed. "Sorry about that."

I rolled my eyes. "And I didn't actually go topless," I whispered, looking at Domino to make sure he didn't hear me.

"I know, but I'm telling everyone you did."

"Gwenny!"

"Kidding. Listen, I'm only calling to wish you good luck. Today's your big brunch day."

I started laying the asparagus out on a sheet pan. "Thanks. I'm actually preparing as we speak."

"OK. Well, good luck. I wish I was there to see you in action. Call me after and tell me how it went."

"Me too. Hey, listen, I need to talk to you about something else. Remember Cade?"

"Yeesss," Gwenny said slowly. I could almost hear her grinning.

"Well, the oth—"

"Hey Em, let's get started, OK?" Domino said.

"Sure, Domino. Hey, Gwenny, I gotta go. I'll tell you everything later."

"Can't wait," Gwenny replied.

I hung up, set the phone aside, and got down to business.

While Domino cut up lemons, I drizzled my asparagus with oil, lightly ground kosher salt and pepper over the top, and slid the pan into the oven. In twenty minutes I would sprinkle it with a layer of parmesan cheese.

"You know, I do my best thinking when I cook," Domino commented.

I glanced at him. Did he know I needed to think about things? The beach incident, Cade, Jeremy, my family.

"Me too," I agreed, arranging the salmon in a couple of roasting pans and dividing the breading evenly among the fillets.

I glanced out the kitchen window, wondering if Cade was already here.

Domino zested lemon into a two-quart pot full of bubbling strawberries, sugar, cornstarch, and water. While it thickened he began browning rice in a large skillet. I heated butter in a saucepan and stirred in onion, celery, and curry powder.

I hope things aren't too awkward with Jeremy coming, too.

Domino turned the heat low and stirred dried cranberries, currants, fig, pear, and sunflower seeds into the browned rice. I grated nutmeg into my buttery concoction and merged it with his.

It shouldn't be awkward, though. It isn't like I'm seriously dating either of them.

Domino checked the asparagus. I tested the salmon with a fork. He handed me a tasting spoon. I adjusted the heat under his strawberry sauce. He put a pinch more salt into the rice. I tossed him a whisk.

Well, I am dating one, sort of, but infatuated with the other.

The timer went off and we both smiled.

"We'll serve up," I told him, "and then start in on the mango mousse."

"Sounds good."

Aunt Tilly swung through the kitchen doors. "Jeremy's here. You got a minute to say hello?"

I glanced at the food we'd just taken from the oven. I really wanted to start plating. *Now, if it were Cade who was here . . .*

"Sure," I told my aunt, knowing that I couldn't be rude.

Jeremy came in then, carrying a bouquet of flowers. "For the chef," he said, presenting them to me.

I smiled, a little surprised, and gave him a hug. "Thank you."

"I know you're busy, so I'll scoot on out. Dinner tomorrow night?"

"Oh, uh, sure." But what if Cade wanted to spend time with me?

He nodded. "Great."

I watched him swing back through the doors and took a whiff of my colorful bouquet. It was the first time a guy had ever given me flowers. They were beautiful.

Domino slid a glass vase of water across the island at me. "Plunk them in there. We've got work to do."

With a smile, I slid the flowers into the water and placed the vase across the kitchen on the windowsill.

Domino and I began plating. I scooped up some jasmine rice with dried fruit and positioned it in the middle of the plate. On top I placed a piece of almond-crusted salmon and drizzled it with strawberry sauce. On either side I positioned spears of parmesan-roasted asparagus and lemon wedges.

"I've already set the usual out on the buffet," Domino told me.

He meant the eggs and bacon, and I knew he'd gotten up extra early to get all that done. What a sweet man.

As we got the plates ready, we laid them out on the counter, and Tilly and Frederick came and got them and delivered them to the guests. While they did their thing with the customers, Domino and I started the final touches on the mango mousse.

I had prepared it the night before and left it to chill in the refrigerator. One by one we pulled out the individual molds and transferred them to pretty little dessert bowls. We garnished each with mango slices, mint leaves, and chocolate wafers.

Tilly and Frederick began bringing in empty plates and taking the mousse out to the diners. As the last mousse was taken off the center island, I took a step back, looked around, and inhaled a deep breath. I'd done it.

I smiled and let out a contented sigh, feeling . . . amazing.

A shadow flickered past the kitchen window. I glanced over to see Cade walk by, and my heart fluttered. He came through the archway that led from the back hallway, carrying a small bunch of wildflowers. He crossed the kitchen to where I stood and handed them to me. "Hey, sorry I'm late. These are for you—as good luck."

I took the bundle of handpicked flowers, tied hodge-podge with a string. Getting the bouquet from Jeremy had been sweet. From Cade, totally, completely unexpected. I didn't know what to do.

"Oh, thanks," I said, smiling. I inadvertently glanced over at Jeremy's gorgeous store-bought bouquet.

Cade followed my glance. "Oh, um," Cade took a step back. "Those are pretty, too."

"Oh, right. Well, um—" I looked up into his blue eyes. "I love wildflowers." I hugged the flowers to my chest. "These mean the world to me."

His lips did that sexy half-tilt thing. "So, is there any food left?"

I nodded, put down the flowers, and grabbed a plate from the cabinet and headed toward the fridge. "Have a seat and I'll fix you a plate."

"Em," Aunt Tilly said, swinging through the doors. "Everyone wants to meet the chef!"

Cade took the plate. "I got this. Go on out and meet your fans, Chef Em."

Chef Em. I liked the sound of that.

I took a deep breath and Cade nodded encouragingly. I smiled back at him and stepped out into the dining room, ready to meet the guests and take in my moment in the culinary spotlight.

***

"My brunch was a total success! I can't believe it," I said to Frederick over a late-day chess game.

We had spent the whole next day together touring the island again on the moped and having a late lunch at an outdoor food shack that served fabulous fish tacos. All in all, a wonderful day.

"Of course it was. I didn't doubt it would be for a minute. No one did. Domino thinks you're really talented."

Frederick was one awesome guy. I considered myself lucky to be related to him. We clicked on this weird level that I'd never been on with anyone else. I wanted to tell him that, but figured it was too mushy of a thing to say. And so I just let our relationship unfold naturally and hoped, *hoped*, that even after I left, Frederick and I would stay in close touch.

"Thanks. Oh, and checkmate," I said, smiling.

"You are getting good!"

I laughed. "OK, next time I'll let you win. But right now, I have to get ready for my date with Jeremy."

Frederick looked at me funny. "You're not going out with Cade?"

"No, why?"

"I heard him mention he was going out, and I just assumed it was with you."

"Oh," I replied as a pang of jealousy hit me.

"Well, have fun with Jeremy."

I smiled and went up to my room to get dressed, trying to ignore the cloud I felt was now hanging over the evening. I quickly changed into a cute skirt and T-shirt, and Jeremy picked me up out front.

Just like before, he was wonderful. Perfect, in fact. I tried to focus all my dating energies on him but unfortunately found my thoughts wandering to Cade. I wondered if I was the first girl he'd ever handpicked flowers for.

"Em?" Jeremy said as we were finishing up our dinner. "I really like you. This has been a lot of fun."

I smiled. "Yeah. It has been." But as I said it, it felt forced coming out of my mouth.

Our bill came and I reached for it. "Want to get ice cream?"

He laughed. "Sure."

We paid and were about to leave when I spotted Cade.

"Hey, guys." Cade said as he walked up to our table.

I glanced up at him, surprised, my stomach fluttering more than it had with Jeremy all night.

Cade held his hand out to Jeremy. "Hey, man."

The two of them launched into a guy conversation—sports this and teams that—while I patiently waited. All the time drinking in the sight of Cade.

"So you here alone?" Jeremy asked.

Cade motioned across the restaurant. "I'm here with Mackenna."

I glanced across the restaurant and recognized Mackenna as the girl he'd been talking to at the juice stand in the farmers' market.

"We were just about to hit the ice-cream shop. You two want to join us?" Jeremy offered.

While my heart did a happy little skip at the thought of hanging out with Cade, I was less than thrilled at the idea of Mackenna hanging on him—and at the idea of me trying to focus on Jeremy.

"Oh." Cade looked at me. "Uh, you sure?"

"Yeah, that'd be great," I extended the offer.

Cade headed off to inform his date, and Jeremy and I met them outside. We walked a block or so down historic Key Street, where an ice-cream shop sat open and doing a booming business.

We took our places in line and made small talk while people placed orders and the line inched forward.

When we got up to the front, Jeremy ordered two scoops

of mint and I ordered one of vanilla. Cade got sinful chocolate and Mackenna ordered fat-free yogurt. Outside, Mackenna and I sat on a bench and the guys stood as we enjoyed our ice creams, the night, and multitude of stars overhead.

I tried not to look at Cade, but in the end gave in and found him staring right at me. He smiled a little when our eyes met, and it shot warmth through my body. My gaze moved to Jeremy to see him carefully studying me.

Immediately, I felt guilty.

"How long are you here?" Mackenna asked me, bringing me from self-shame.

"Just till the end of the month," I told her.

"I heard your brunch was fantastic," she complimented me.

"Thanks." I liked Mackenna. She seemed sweet. "How'd you hear that?"

"Cade told me."

"Oh." I glanced up at Cade again, and he gave me one of those half-smiles.

Mackenna checked her watch. "Sorry, guys. Gotta go."

"I'll walk you home," Cade told her, and turned to me. "I'm coming by the Pepper after to get the van. Got early errands in the morning."

I nodded, hoping beyond hopes I would see him later. I watched them head down Key Street before turning my attention back to Jeremy. He was studying me, like he knew I'd rather be walking with Cade right then instead of finishing ice cream with him. And that made me feel horrible.

"Ready?" he asked, tossing the rest of his cone in a nearby garbage can.

I nodded.

He took me home. We exchanged a quick kiss. He said he'd talk to me later. I planned to call him first thing in the morning. If anything, to prove I wasn't a complete jerk. I liked Jeremy. He'd been nothing but great to me, but my heart just wasn't in it.

As he pulled away, I turned toward the Pepper House and something caught my eye. I squinted into the shadows and made out a person's figure. "Cade?"

"It's Sid," Cade's dad said, stepping from the shadows.

My heart paused. "Sid?"

"I didn't mean to scare you." He smiled a little. "How are you, Em?"

"I'm fine." I looked around, confused and a little concerned. "Are you OK? What are you doing here?"

He gave a guilty shrug. "Waiting for Cade, actually. I thought for sure I'd see him." He paused. "I'm his father."

"Yes, I know."

Sid appeared a little surprised. "He told you that, did he?"

He doesn't talk about you, I almost responded. "No, Aunt Tilly told me."

"Ah. He doesn't talk about me," Sid noted, as if he had read my thoughts.

"No, not really." I felt terrible admitting it to him.

Sid came closer. "So, how is he?"

I smiled through a sigh, hating that he had to ask a stranger that question. "He's good, Sid." *What happened between you two?* I wanted to ask but instead said, "He said he'd be here later. I'm not sure when, though."

"Well . . . tell him I came by, I guess."

"I will," I reassured him.

I turned to go into the house just as Cade pulled up on a moped. He cut the engine and took off his helmet. "Sid? What are you doing here?"

Chapter Fourteen

"I just wanted to see you," Sid replied.

"Well, you've seen me." Cade got off the bike.

I stood still, silent, wanting to leave but not wanting to disrupt their conversation.

Sid didn't say anything for a couple of seconds. "You're still wearing that, huh?"

I peered through the shadows at Cade and saw the small ring hanging from the chain around his neck. He took a deep breath, and the ring caught the glow of the Pepper House's exterior lights as he tucked it into his shirt.

"Do you visit her?" Sid asked.

Cade didn't answer that question; instead, he just studied his dad. "Do you?"

Sid swallowed. "Every day that I'm here," he whispered.

Silence. Neither one of them spoke a word. I stood there on the driveway, my gaze going between the two of them, wondering what had happened to make them so distant from each other. Who were they were referring to? And what was the significance of that ring around Cade's neck?

The more silence that ticked by, the more uncomfortable I felt. "Um . . ." I took a step back. "I should leave you two alone."

"No, you don't have to go," Cade said to me.

I stopped backing away. I couldn't tell if he really wanted me to stay, but I didn't want to make a scene.

"I know I screwed up," Sid mumbled with true humility in his tone.

Cade huffed. "Little late for that, don't you think?"

"No," Sid said.

Cade folded his arms over his chest. "What are you doing here? What do you expect? What do you want from me?"

Sid swallowed again, and even in the night's darkness, I could make out the anguish on his face. "Cade . . ."

Cade let out a long sigh. "Just get on your boat, Sid, and sail away. That's what you want to do anyway."

Slowly, Sid nodded, then turned and disappeared down the driveway.

Neither Cade nor I moved, spoke, or did anything for a minute. My thoughts reeled with what I'd witnessed. Cade's sadness. Sid's humility. The tension between them. I didn't know what to think. And none of it was my business.

But . . . everyone deserved forgiveness, right? Clearly, that was what Sid desperately wanted and needed.

I cleared my throat. "I think I'm going to go inside now."

Cade turned his eyes to me, as if just remembering I was there. "Don't go thinking you know anything from what you just saw."

The agitation in his voice took me off guard. He was the one who had told me I didn't have to go.

I shrugged. "It's none of my business."

"You're right, it's none of your business," he stonily agreed.

I blinked, feeling sad for them. I also felt a spark of irritation that Cade seemed to be taking his frustration out on me. "I know. I'm just going to go to bed."

Cade took a step toward me. "I don't want you telling anybody about this. This is my issue."

I just stood there, staring at him, dumbfounded. "I won't, Cade." I turned to go. "Good night."

"Where are you going?"

I turned back around. "I just said—to bed."

He clenched his jaw.

"Cade, what do you want from me?" I asked, confused.

He took another step toward me. A couple of seconds passed and his shoulders dropped. "I don't know," he whispered.

I stared up into his confused eyes and wished I could make his sadness go away. "Cade, I'm sorry."

He reached his hand out and I automatically took it. He moved closer, putting us just a few inches apart. We stood studying each other's face. I wished I knew what he was thinking.

Slowly, he lowered his head and gave me a very soft kiss that gradually turned into something deeper.

I fell into the kiss, wanting more. Then, all of a sudden, he pulled back. "Sorry," he mumbled. "I shouldn't have done that."

I didn't have a response to that. *I* wasn't sorry.

"I'm . . . I'm just going to go," he said.

I didn't know what to say.

I watched as Cade walked over to the van, got in, and drove off.

I just stood there, staring into the night, completely confused.

After a few moments, I headed in and went up to bed. I barely slept the whole night, totally sidetracked by what had happened. Sid showing up, his argument with Cade, me standing awkwardly by. Cade telling me not to go, then taking out his irritation on me. The feel of his lips as he kissed me. Then the apology. *Why* the apology?

Aunt Tilly startled me out of sleep the next morning when she knocked on my door. "Em? You coming down?"

"Yeah," I sighed, rubbing my eyes. "In a bit."

"Everything OK?"

No, not really. I had no clue what to say to Cade when I saw him next. I didn't know if he even wanted to see me. "I'll be down it a bit," I repeated. "That is, if you don't mind?"

"Not at all."

I heard her walk away. Another hour came and went. I ignored Gwenny's call when it came. I didn't call Jeremy like I had promised myself I would.

All I could think about was Cade. I replayed the events of the previous night over and over and over again in my head.

Another hour ticked by and my stomach began to grumble. I swung my legs over the side of my bed and sat for a minute gazing out my window. I wondered what Cade was doing right at that moment. Was he downstairs working? He said he had early morning errands.

A knock came on my door, and I turned to see Aunt Tilly slide in. She sat down beside me. "If you haven't figured it out by now, I'm a good listener. And I'd like to think I give OK advice."

Unexpected tears welled in my eyes. It was embarrassing, really. I'd never been the type to cry. My mother and grandmother didn't have much patience for tears.

To her credit, Aunt Tilly didn't console me. Thank God. It probably would have made me cry even more. Instead, she lay back on my bed and stared at the ceiling fan as it slowly circled.

A few minutes passed, and, still looking out the window, I got control of my emotions. With a deep breath, I turned to her. "I don't know what to do."

She kept staring at the ceiling fan. "Is this about Cade?"

I rolled my eyes with a nod. "Yes."

A small smile curved her lips. "I could tell you two had something for each other."

"What?"

Aunt Tilly looked at me then. "I've known Cade a long time. And I've *never* seen him so affected by a girl until you."

My heart paused a beat as my aunt's words echoed through my head. I waited for her to elaborate, but when she didn't, I asked, "What do you mean?"

"Oh, Em," Aunt Tilly sighed, sitting up on my bed. "If you

could see the way he looks at you when you're not looking. Among other things."

My heart skipped again. "What other things?" I asked a little too quickly.

Smiling, she reached over and cupped my cheek in her hand. "Em, that's for you to figure out."

I knew she was right.

Grabbing my pillow, I tucked it against my body and turned on my bed to face my aunt. "I just don't know what to do. I've never met a guy like Cade. He seems to bring out just about every thought and emotion in me."

She smiled a little at that.

"And when he smiles in that sexy little way . . ." My eyes widened. "I can't believe I just said that to you."

Aunt Tilly laughed as I proceeded to completely turn red.

"Frederick's dad was that way. That man could turn me inside out. Sometimes I felt like I was on a roller coaster and other times I was the most peaceful I'd ever been."

I sighed. "And then there's Jeremy. He's so sweet, but every time I'm with him, Cade seems to enter my mind. It makes me feel horrible about myself."

Aunt Tilly smoothed her hand over my head. "Don't feel horrible. It's life. You're learning. Trust your instincts. You know right from wrong. And if you make a mistake, don't beat yourself up about it."

"Can't you just tell me what to do?"

She gave me a peck on the cheek and got up. "Sorry, hon, no can do. I will tell you, though, that Jeremy deserves honesty. Don't lead him on. It's not fair to him."

I nodded, loving the comfort and support Aunt Tilly so generously gave. And to think I'd only known her for a few weeks. It was so hard to believe. It seemed like I'd known her a lifetime.

Aunt Tilly headed for my door. "Anytime you want to talk, don't be afraid to come to me. There's no topic off limits with me."

Actually, there was—the feud with my family—but I didn't want to ruin the moment.

* * *

I spent the rest of the day by myself. I took a nap in the hammock. I logged onto Frederick's laptop and answered all the e-mails that had accumulated in my in-box. I made a big bowl of buttery popcorn and read a romance novel I found on the bookshelf. I even did some reading for my law internship. It was good to take time to myself. By the next morning I was completely determined to enjoy every moment of the new day.

Domino put me in charge of making cranberry-walnut pancakes. Even though I was still a bit preoccupied with thoughts of Cade, I did think to sprinkle in some nutmeg and add a dash of orange extract. I was glad I did because the guests raved. It was the orange extract. It added a little secret oomph to the cranberries, marrying the flavors perfectly with the walnuts.

"Sweetie, you never cease to amaze me," Domino commented while we cleaned up.

I smiled, and a few seconds later nonchalantly asked, "Have you, uh, seen Cade around?"

"Tilly said he was by before the sun even came up. Did all his chores. Left a note in the office to say he'd be back tomorrow."

"Oh." I tried not to show my disappointment.

The morning came and went. I helped Beth a bit with the housekeeping. I played a game of chess with Frederick. But my brain just wasn't in things.

I tried calling Jeremy, got his voice mail, and left a message. The next time I saw him, I definitely planned to clear things up.

Aunt Tilly was right. It wasn't fair to Jeremy to be half into him.

"Mind if I borrow one of the mopeds?" I asked Aunt Tilly.

With nothing on my agenda for the rest of the day, I thought I'd ride around the island and see where things took me. I had no destination. I just wanted to feel the warm air on my face.

I rode along the coastal highway. I passed the marina and saw Sid's boat, but not him. I puttered past the surfing beach, remembering my lesson with Cade. I went to the center of the island and slowly motored through the downtown area. I even went out to the airport and sat for a while watching planes come and go.

On the way home, I headed to the cemetery and found Cade bent over the same grave I'd seen Sid standing over a week earlier.

Cade looked up when I cut the moped's engine. He made no expression, said nothing, and went back to looking at the grave.

Slowly, I approached him until I was standing right beside

him, looking down at the headstone. I read DANA FARRELL etched into the granite.

"My mom," Cade stated simply.

I nodded.

He reached inside his T-shirt and pulled out the chain he always wore. "This was her ring."

I smiled a little, not really knowing what to say but not wanting to lose this special moment with him. I wanted us to talk, but I didn't want to push him.

"My dad's an alcoholic," he stated matter-of-factly.

"Oh." I looked at him as he stared at his mother's grave. I slowly reached over and took his hand. He didn't pull away, but he didn't grasp my hand in return.

Some time passed as we silently stood there staring at his mom's grave, both lost in thought. I wasn't sure when it happened, but I was suddenly aware that he had repositioned our hands and linked fingers with me. I'd held hands with guys before, but something was different this time. I felt more of a connection, like we needed each other's hand.

"Will you tell me about her?" I quietly asked.

Smiling a little, he sat down on the ground, pulling me down with him.

"She was beautiful," Cade finally said. "Intelligent. Adventurous. Bighearted. She'd do anything for anyone. And she had the biggest smile you've ever seen." Cade chuckled a little at the memory. "Her one mistake in life was falling in love with Sid."

The bitterness in his voice when he said his dad's name made my throat constrict.

"They were high school sweethearts," Cade continued. "He was a train wreck even back then. But Mom was completely devoted to him. She would have followed him to the ends of the earth. She defended him to the whole town when everyone told her Sid was a loser. She loved him. And that was that."

He paused and shook his head.

"How did she die?" I asked.

Cade turned and looked straight at me with eyes devoid of emotion. "She drowned while out sailing with Sid."

Chapter Fifteen

I sat very still as Cade's words sank in.

The longer I sat, the harder I felt my heart thud. "Cade . . ."

He let out a humorless chuckle and looked away from me and back to his mom's grave.

I swallowed, wishing I knew what to say. "Wh-what happened?" I whispered.

"Sid got drunk," Cade said in a barely audible voice. "Decided to go sailing. Mom went with him. Only one of them came back."

"Where were you?" I whispered.

Cade didn't answer at first and instead kept staring at his mom's grave. Eventually, he took his hand from mine to scrub his face.

I'd forgotten we'd been holding hands.

"I was only ten at the time," he croaked. "I yelled at my mom not to go. She didn't listen. I yelled at my mom to take me with her. She didn't listen . . ."

He lapsed into silence, his face covered by his hands. He was trying so hard to control his emotions.

I put my hand on his back.

"Mom was good friends with your aunt," he mumbled into his palms. "She dropped me off at the Pepper House on the way to the marina . . . That was the last time I ever saw her."

"Oh, Cade." I scooted closer to him on the ground and wrapped my arms around his shoulders.

He didn't take his hands off his face as I hugged him. "Sid came back weeks later. Mom wasn't with him." Cade inhaled a deep breath. "He said he was drunk and fell overboard. She dove in to save him. Only . . . she got swept away in the current."

"Oh my gosh," I whispered.

He looked at me then. "Your aunt Tilly took me in, did you know that? The room you're in now used to be my room."

"I didn't know."

"Sid quickly reappeared and then proceeded to disappear again. A whole year went by before I saw him. And it's been like that ever since. Almost as if I'd lost both of them." Cade turned away from me and stared into the trees that bordered the cemetery. "Do you think he's bothered to give your aunt Tilly money for me? No. He'd make his annual visit, stay for a few days, and head back out on his boat." Cade let out another humorless chuckle. "He did at least manage to remember to thank your aunt a time or two."

It struck me then how bitter Cade sounded. Bitter—a word I'd always reserved for older people who had been through a lot. Cade was only nineteen, but he'd already experienced a lifetime of hurt.

Silence stretched between us as we sat on the ground at his mom's grave. I stared at the side of his face, and the anguish I saw there hit me straight in the gut.

I moved so that I was sitting in front of him. I stared into his tormented face. I took in the creases of his brow, his blue eyes, the blond stubble on his cheeks, and the hard set of his jaw.

I leaned forward and pressed a tender kiss to his cheek. "I'm so sorry, Cade." I wished I had something more significant to say, but it was all I could think of. I hoped he could tell just how much I meant it.

He brought his gaze to mine and his brow relaxed little by little as he stared at me. I watched myriad expressions cross his face—perplexed, curious, questioning . . . and vulnerable—all things I'd rather see than the anguish of before.

"Will you come somewhere with me?" he asked with lingering hurt in his voice.

I smiled a little. "Sure."

He had no moped, so we doubled on mine. He drove us down the hill from the cemetery and straight through the center of town. Cade cut down a side street and came to a stop in front of a glass-blowing shop. He killed the engine and climbed off.

I was dying to ask him what we were doing at a glass-blowing shop, but kept my lips closed.

He didn't go into the shop but instead headed down a side alley. I followed him all the way to the end, where he opened and walked straight through an unlocked door.

The door led into a small hall, with another door to the right and one on the left. Cade turned the knob on the left and stepped into a dim room. I followed, looking all around as I stepped inside. Driftwood furniture, cream-painted walls, hardwood floors.

"This looks just like the Pepper House," I commented.

Cade smiled, the first one I'd seen from him in a while. "Your aunt helped me decorate it."

My eyes widened in surprise. "This is your place?"

I turned a slow circle, taking it all in again. "I thought when you move out on your own, you're supposed to do things your style."

Cade shrugged. "This is my style." He was back to being the Cade I knew—not the Cade from the cemetery.

I laughed a little. "Well, when I finally get my own place, I'm so not decorating it my parents' way."

"And what way is that?"

"Delicate, fancy, expensive—also known as uncomfortable. It's just not me."

Cade looked me up and down. "Yeah, delicate and fancy is definitely not you."

"Hey! What's that supposed to mean?" I might have been offended if it weren't for the teasing note in his voice.

Cade laughed. "I just mean when I first met you I would've definitely pegged you for the fancy, stuffy scene. But now"—he shrugged—"you're different."

"Different?"

"More down to earth."

That's funny. I didn't think I'd changed at all. "You just didn't know me. I really haven't changed."

He nodded. "Yeah, you have."

I thought about it for a few seconds. I felt more like myself at that moment than I ever had. I was cooking on a regular basis. I didn't worry about being proper and poised day in and day out. I was comfortable, content.

"So how about the grand tour?" he invited.

"Sure."

He pointed to the wall on his right. "On the other side of that wall is the glass-blowing shop. My mom worked there pretty much since the day she could work. She loved the art. She even had an apprenticeship with the blower. A lot of things they carried were hers." Cade smiled a little. "I spent a lot of time in there."

"Do you have any of her pieces?"

"Oh, yeah. I've got them packed and stored at the Pepper House."

"Will you show me sometime?" I asked, realizing I wanted to see this side of him. Where he came from. I wanted to know as much about Cade Farrell as I could.

With a curious half-smile, he studied me for a few seconds.

I looked right and then left. "What?"

He shook his head. "Nothing. It's just no one has ever asked me that before."

"Oh." I wasn't sure if that was a good thing or not.

Cade turned away from the wall that separated him from his mom's history. He pointed across the room to a mini-kitchenette. "The kitchen." He pointed to his futon couch. "My couch-slash-bed." He pointed to two oversized, driftwood chairs with a table separating them. "Guest seating." He pointed to an old stereo perched in the corner. "Music." He pointed to long cabinets that stretched from the floor to the ceiling. "Storage." He pointed to the hardwood floor. "Floor."

Then I saw his lips twitch and I laughed. "OK, I get it. This is it."

He headed into the kitchen. "Drink?"

"Sure."

He rifled around in the refrigerator, brought out two sodas, and motioned me over to the futon to sit.

For a few quiet seconds we sat sipping our sodas.

"Thanks," he finally said, "for back there at the cemetery."

"Oh." I smiled a little. "You're welcome."

"I'm a basket case, huh?" Cade huffed out a laugh that held no humor. "Drunk dad, dead mom . . ."

I looked at him. "Cade, we all have our troubles. And, no, you're not a basket case."

He nodded and took a sip of his soda. I stared at him, willing him to talk about our two kisses. Wanting to know what was going on with us. Instead, he said, "And what troubles do you have, Em? Seems like you had a pretty good upbringing. A little stuffy for my taste, but—"

I chuckled at the stuffy comment. Cade had no idea. "I have had it good," I agreed with him. I realized then how different he and I were. I had had nothing but stability and consistency, and he'd had Sid's alcoholism and abandonment and the death of his mom.

"There's a lot more to having it good than schools and clothes," Cade wisely observed. "What good are all those material things if you don't appreciate them, you know? I'm sure you know people like that."

I'd never heard it put quite that way before, but it rang true.

Cade studied me. "Something tells me your parents have very high expectations that you've spent a lifetime scrambling to meet." He touched his finger to my chest. "Inside here is the person you really want to be. I think you just don't how to be her without disappointing your parents."

I stared at Cade, feeling the warmth of his finger on my chest, his words soaking in. Nobody had ever pegged me so clearly. He was right, I was so focused on what I was supposed to do and be, I couldn't see through to my true self.

I let out a nervous laugh. "Ever thought of being a psychologist?"

He shrugged and took his finger back. "Nah. I just read people well."

This side of Cade was so surprising. He was so much more thoughtful and intelligent than I had given him credit for. "You're right, my parents and grandmother have very high expectations of me. They expect me to be a certain way, and

that's the way I try to be." I shrugged. "I've never thought
about doing anything differently."

"Sounds controlling."

"It can be," I agreed. More than he knew. "And you? Do
you know where you're headed in life?"

Cade sipped his soda. "I think so. Honestly, I'm not too
worried about it. I trust that things will fall into place as they
may. I like to dabble in many things."

"Is that code for 'unfocused'?" I joked.

He laughed. "Sounds good to me."

I knew he was kidding. I remembered what I had thought
the first time I saw him. *Sexy loser.* Now that I knew him better,
something about him told me he'd be very successful someday.
"So no life plan?"

He winked. "I'm working on it."

I thought about how Cade had had to grow up so quickly.
He probably already had things figured out. He just wasn't
ready to share that side of himself yet.

I envied him. The freedom. Knowing who he was and what
he wanted. The comfort he obviously felt with himself.

Reaching over, he took a lock of my long hair and ran it
through his fingers. He twirled it, studying me, and the more
he studied me, the deeper I felt my heart thud.

"You'd like my sister," I told him. Why I thought of her at
that particular second, I didn't know.

"Yeah?"

I nodded, my brain hazy with the feel of him tugging on my
hair. "She's wonderful. I'd love for everyone here to meet her.
Her free spirit would fit right in."

He nodded and smiled at me. After a few seconds, he looked down. "So," he started, and I looked at him expectantly. "About the other day—"

Someone banged on his door, snapping both of us from the moment.

Cade got up and went to answer it.

An elderly lady stood on the other side. "Cade, hon, my toilet's leaking again. Mind taking a look?"

"Uh, sure." He turned to me. "My neighbor. This'll take a while. You can take the moped back."

"Oh." I pushed to my feet, somewhat reluctantly. "OK."

Cade headed out his door and I grabbed the moped keys off his counter. I didn't want to go. I wanted to stay. I wanted him to keep playing with my hair. I wanted to keep talking. Most of all, I wanted him to kiss me again.

Chapter Sixteen

The next morning I moved around my room getting ready for the day. I knew it was silly to think, but somehow my room seemed different now that I knew Cade had slept and lived in it.

My phone buzzed:

WHAT'S 4 B-FAST THIS A.M.?

I texted Gwenny back:

DON'T KNOW. A LITTLE PREOCCUPIED.

FOUND OUT A LOT ABOUT CADE YESTERDAY.

OH?

I'LL CALL LATER. 2 MUCH 2 TELL NOW.

DEFINITELY CALL ME!

I smiled as I closed my phone and slipped on my flip-flops. I took one last glance around my room and made my way down the hall.

Frederick was already up, stretched across his bed reading. "Morning," I greeted him, and he looked up with a smile.

Aunt Tilly's door stood open and her bed was already made. The gauzy canopy that draped her bed billowed a little on the breeze. I peeked my head inside her door to see she'd already left.

Halfway down the back stairs, I glanced out the window to see Cade shirtless and bent over one of the mopeds. Immediately, I recalled when I'd first arrived. I'd stood at the same window looking out at a shirtless Cade as he'd tended to a bush. I would have never thought we'd have such a connection.

The day before in his apartment had ended too soon. I could've sat there for hours talking, drinking in his blue eyes, falling a little harder for him.

As Cade had suggested, I'd headed home, thinking of him the entire way. Thinking of him as I ate dinner, as I got ready for bed, as I lay trying to go to sleep, as I woke up . . .

Domino was in the kitchen pulling stuff out of the refrigerator. "Hey, sweetie. We're going Southern today with biscuits and gravy."

"My thighs are bigger just thinking about it," I joked, and Domino laughed.

Domino and I spread out to work. As I went through the routine of mixing, rolling, and cutting biscuits, I let my thoughts drift back to Cade.

There was a deeper side to him that surprised me, delighted me, and intrigued me. I wanted to know more—and I wanted to know where we stood.

Breakfast came and went. Aunt Tilly and Frederick served

the guests. Beth showed up at some point to snag some food before diving into her chores. Domino and I cleaned the kitchen, and just as I was placing the last of the leftover biscuits into a basket, Cade walked in.

"Smells good," he commented.

I tried for casual. "Thanks."

"Help yourself," Domino told him, and walked out, leaving Cade and me alone.

Cade reached into the basket, grabbed a biscuit, and took a bite. He didn't say anything, and the silence started making me a little self-conscious.

I cleared my throat. "Biscuit's good?"

He nodded, took another bite, and just watched me.

I didn't know what to expect, but this awkwardness was not it. "Thirsty?"

Cade nodded.

I concentrated on keeping my hands steady as I went to the cabinet and got a glass. I went to the refrigerator and got the milk. I set both on the counter and glanced up to see him chewing, still watching me.

I poured the milk, put the jug back, placed the glass in front of Cade, and busied myself with wiping a counter that really didn't need to be wiped.

What was going on? Why wasn't he saying anything?

I heard him slide the glass from the counter and glanced up. He took a drink, still watching me. I smiled a little and dug around in my brain for something to say, but came up with nothing.

Frederick came in. "Hey, Cade."

"Hey."

Frederick put some dirty plates in the sink. "I'm heading to Cottage One to help Beth. Oh, Em, Jeremy called," he told me before heading out.

On the Jeremy comment, I immediately glanced at Cade.

He took another gulp of his milk. "So Jeremy, huh?"

I shrugged. "He's a nice guy."

"Are you . . . are you guys like dating or something?"

I swallowed and answered honestly. "We've been on a couple of dates."

He walked his empty glass over to the sink and slipped it into the soapy water. "What would you say if I asked you out?"

My stomach did a big slow whirl. "I'd say yes."

"Tomorrow?"

I smiled. "OK."

He smiled back and motioned to the dirty dishes. "Need help?"

I turned to the sink and the dishes. "No, it's OK, I've got it." I dug both hands in and started washing. I scrubbed exactly one plate before I realized Cade hadn't moved from beside me. Actually, he'd moved a little closer. Close enough that I felt the warmth coming off his body.

I tried to concentrate on washing, but my mind was focused solely on Cade.

"Thank you," he murmured, "again. For yesterday."

I glanced over my shoulder and up into eyes gentled by emotion. I didn't know what I had expected, but this was not it. "You're welcome," I murmured back.

Cade drew closer and pressed a soft kiss to my cheek. "I'll see you tomorrow," he whispered, and took a step back. "We'll leave right after breakfast."

I nodded. "OK."

And then he was gone.

I couldn't say how long I stood staring at the spot where he'd been standing, going over the entire thing in my head. I couldn't say how long it took my body to cool off from his warmth. I couldn't say, but the buzzing of the doorbell had me snapping out of it.

Wiping my hands on a dish towel, I made my way from the kitchen and into the dining room. A glance out the back window confirmed where Aunt Tilly and Domino were—standing by the bay, talking about something. I slung the towel over my shoulder and continued on into the living room.

A tall man stood by the chessboard studying the move Frederick and I had last left off with. He wore khaki pants, a white polo, and a blue sports jacket. He had neat, short salt-and-pepper hair with more salt than pepper. I guessed him to be in his forties or fifties. Old enough to be my dad, for sure, but I thought he was good-looking. For an older guy. And something about him seemed familiar.

"Hi," I greeted him.

He turned. "Oh, hello." He nodded to the door. "I rang a few times but no one answered, so I let myself in. I hope that's OK."

I smiled. "Sure. May I help you?"

He approached me with his hand out to shake. "Harold Lemley."

Harold Lemley. His name seemed familiar. I circled it around in my brain, trying to remember where I'd heard it. . . .

"I have a reservation," he continued. "Are you Tilly?"

"No, Tilly's my aunt. I'm Em. Nice to meet you. Welcome. Where are you from?"

"Originally Sacramento. But now I find my home wherever my boat and the water take me."

"Your boat." It dawned on me where I might have seen him. "Oh, are you the owner of that large yacht that was at the marina?"

He nodded. "I am."

"I was wondering if you were a movie star or something."

Harold laughed at that. "Hardly."

I smiled. "You've got quite the bodyguard, did you know that?"

"My what?"

I told him about my walk down the dock weeks ago and that big man standing guard in front of the yacht.

Harold chuckled. "That's my younger brother. He's my security. Sometimes he takes his job a little too seriously. We've had problems with vandals over the past months, and so he's a little overprotective. I do apologize for that."

I waved it off. "That's OK." I was dying to ask him what he did for a living such that he could afford to travel around on a big yacht, but I knew that was a rude question. "So you've decided to be landlocked for a while?"

"Yes, my boat needs some repairs and so here I am."

"Em?" Aunt Tilly yelled my name.

"In here," I called back.

She bustled in. "Beth needs—" She came to an abrupt stop. "Oh . . ." she looked at Mr. Harold Lemley. "Hi."

He smiled. "Hello."

"I'll go see if Beth needs any help," I said, leaving them. "It was nice meeting you, Mr. Lemley."

"Likewise."

While they stood talking, I left, pondering his name. *Harold Lemley*. Something *definitely* sounded familiar about it.

Chapter Seventeen

The next morning Jeremy called and told me he just wanted to be friends. I should have been relieved, as that's what I wanted to say to him, but the whole thing left me feeling weird.

Weird like I had let too much time pass and should've been the one to call him, not the other way around.

Weird like I had somehow messed up and lost a friend.

He told me he wanted to stay in touch, but still, the whole thing just didn't feel right. I didn't feel good about myself. I felt like I should have been more honest with him.

"Who took your last lollipop?" Aunt Tilly asked, coming into my room.

I halfheartedly chuckled at her silly remark. "Do I look that bummed?"

She nodded. "Want to talk about it?"

I sat down on the edge of my bed and told her about the phone call. "I feel badly. I didn't treat him right. And now I have a date with Cade. How can I go and enjoy myself with him while I'm feeling guilty about Jeremy?"

Tilly sat down beside me. "As hard as you try, Em, you're not perfect. You're going to make mistakes. Let some time pass, then give Jeremy a call and apologize. It's the right thing to do. Just don't beat yourself up over all this."

I nodded.

Tilly got up. "Now, go have fun with Cade and worry about this later."

Trying to shake off my melancholy, I headed downstairs. "Hey, Domino," I said as I·stepped into the kitchen. "Do you know where Cade is?"

"Well, good morning to you too, sweetie."

Playfully, I rolled my eyes.

"Cade hasn't shown up yet." Domino waved a metal whisk at me. "But I heard you two have a hot date."

I blushed a little. "I don't know what you're talking about."

Domino laughed. "Please, nothing's a secret around here."

"Do you know what we're doing?" I asked. "Where we're going?"

Domino drew an X with his finger over his lips. "Top-secret information you're asking for there." He tossed an apple at me. "Now, get busy. The sooner you get done with breakfast, the sooner you're out of here."

Methodically I cored apples, prepping them for the baking,

thinking through everything. With each apple, I felt a little better and a little better. Tilly was right. I wasn't perfect. And I shouldn't beat myself up over Jeremy.

I helped Domino prep the rest of the meal, then assisted Frederick and Aunt Tilly with serving the guests. As I was wringing out a dishrag, Cade appeared in the doorway. "Done?"

I nodded and untied my apron. "Where are we going? What should I pack?"

"Nothing. I've already got everything. Just make sure you have your suit on."

With good-byes to everyone, we headed out the front to the van and climbed in. There were a couple of duffel bags in the back and a cooler. But everything was closed up, so I still had no idea what Cade had planned.

"What's in the duffels?" I asked, so excited at the intrigue I nearly bounced in my seat.

Cade laughed. "You'll find out."

"It's just no one's ever planned a surprise day for me before."

"No one's ever surprised you before?" He cranked the engine. "Then I'd say you're definitely due."

Come to think of it, I always had a game plan. I always knew what I was doing, what my family expected me to do. I'd lived more in the moment here than I had in my entire life.

Go figure. Me, Elizabeth Margaret, being spontaneous.

Cade pulled out onto the coastal highway. "What are you laughing at?"

"Me." And that made me laugh even more. "I love this spontaneity. My life is way too scripted."

Cade looked at me, amused. "Well, you should feel honored."

"Why's that?"

"I normally *don't* have a script, so to say I planned a day is saying something."

I propped my arm in the open window. "I do feel honored. Looks like both of us are stepping out of our usual selves for the day."

He smiled. "Looks like."

We rode on in silence for a few minutes with the windows down and the ocean breeze flowing in. We passed the marina and I couldn't help myself glancing over to see if Sid's boat was there.

It wasn't.

We passed the spot where we'd gone surfing, and a few minutes later we pulled off to the right and parked alongside the coastal highway.

Cade cut the engine. "First stop," he said, opening the driver's door.

I climbed out of my side of the van and stood for a second staring straight down. We were on a ledge that seemed to drop straight into the ocean. The ocean rolled and crashed into rocks, spraying saltwater up and out.

"It's beautiful," I said.

Cade took my hand. "You haven't seen anything yet."

He led me past the van, ducked between two palm trees,

and stepped onto a rough-cut trail bordered by wild bushes.

I surveyed the steep trail as it wound down, a little hesitant of the incline.

Cade gave my hand a little tug. "Come on."

I nodded and followed him down, using the bushes to steady myself and trying to take in the scenery at the same time. Greenery covered the whole ledge. So thick, in fact, it was nearly impossible to see anything else. Underbrush so tall I saw only glimpses of the ocean through it.

"All this green reminds me of Ireland. Gwenny and I toured this old university and we were amazed at how much ivy and green covered everything. It was so beautiful."

"It is great," Cade agreed, stepping down the trail. "What was the name of the university?"

"I don't remember."

"Does it look anything like Harvard?"

"Harvard?"

"Yeah, Tilly told me you're going there?"

"Yes, I'm going to be a lawyer and work at my dad's firm." It was my standard answer. One my dad had been telling people since forever. An answer I naturally gave too.

"Really."

His reply wasn't a question, but a statement. I was used to people being impressed, not *unimpressed* with my career aspirations. Or, I should say, my *dad's* career aspirations.

"What do you *really* want to do?" He looked over his shoulder, giving me one of those sexy half-smiles.

"I . . . I really want to be a chef."

He rounded an overhanging bush, holding it out of the way for me. "Yeah, I can totally see that."

My heart skipped a little with glee. "Really?"

Cade gave one affirmative nod. "Yep, your food is something else."

I laughed at that. "Reality is, though, I'll be a lawyer."

He stopped walking and turned to me. "Why? Because someone told you so?"

"Well . . . yes, actually." It felt stupid to admit that. "It's already paid for and everything."

Cade gave me an incredulous look. "Oh, really. It's paid for. As in your dad has already written a check to some university for umpteen years of studies."

"Well, no, of course not. I mean, it's in an account and earmarked for my college."

Cade's brows lifted. "Earmarked? Are you listening to yourself? Em, it's great—*wonderful*, in fact—that your parents set aside money for you and college. But if you don't want to go to a regular university, then don't go. If you want to go to culinary school, go."

I sighed. "But they won't pay for culinary school."

"Then pay for it yourself."

"But . . ." I stared at him, and he stared back. And the more I stared the more I realized he was right. If I truly wanted to be a chef, I needed to make it happen. College fund or no college fund. "But they'll be upset. It's not what they want for me. It's not what they've planned for me. I'm valedictorian, for God's sake. Valedictorians can't be chefs."

"Why not?"

"Well . . ." I thought about that for a few seconds and could come up with no solid reason. Who said valedictorians couldn't be chefs?

"Sooner or later you're going to figure out your life is your life. You can't please everybody. Now's the time for you to make a change before you're too far into the whole law thing."

Cade was right. I needed to stop trying to be someone I didn't really want to be.

"Tilly told me once you can't make others happy until you're happy," Cade said. "I really believe in that."

"Is that why you do things the way you want to do them?"

"Darn right." He leaned in. "Valedictorian, huh? Pretty hot."

I blushed at his comment.

Cade pushed a shrub aside. "We're here," he announced.

Ducking around, I stepped through and onto a very small patch of sand. I turned and looked all the way up to where we'd come from. "Wow, I didn't realize we'd come that far!"

Cade nodded. He took off his shoes and tied them to the top of a bush. I followed his lead, taking off mine and handing them over for him to tie off too.

He took my hand. "Come on."

We inched along the tiny beach with the water nearly touching our toes. One big boulder sat up ahead, so large it blocked us from continuing on. Between the boulder and the wall of the ledge I made out a tiny sliver of an opening.

Still holding my hand, Cade stepped sideways into the opening and I followed.

I'd never been scared of the dark, but we had just stepped

into what was, hands-down, the darkest place I'd ever been.

Gripping his hand tighter, I blindly followed him. "Where are we going?"

"Scared?" his voice echoed around me.

"No." *Yes.*

My bare toes squished in the watery sand and I prayed I didn't step on some weird poisonous sea creature. A soft spray of water hit my face, and I flinched.

"You OK?"

"Mm-hm."

No sooner did my mumbled response echo around us than I saw a light up ahead.

I held Cade's hand, following him, staring at the light. And a few seconds later we stepped from the dark tunnel and into the most beautiful place I'd seen in my entire life.

Chapter Eighteen

"It's beautiful," I whispered, staring straight ahead, unable to say anything more than that.

Still holding my hand, Cade led me from the dark tunnel and into an underground room filled with a crystal-clear blue lake. Sunshine streaming in from above sent sparkles of light dancing over the aqua surface. In the center of the lake sat a tiny sandy island. A pebbled path outlined the lake. Beyond the path the walls of the cave led fifty feet up to where an opening framed the sky and sun.

Cade turned to me with a smile. "It's amazing, isn't it?"

I simply nodded, so stunned at the natural wonder in front of me.

"It's fed from below. The ocean comes through a tunnel beneath us and fills the lake."

I looked around. "How did you find this place?"

He smiled. "My mom."

I studied the lake. "I don't remember reading about this. And I read *everything* there was about this island when I found out I was coming here."

Cade took his shirt off. "We locals like to keep a few secrets to ourselves. And it doesn't always have water. I suppose that's why it doesn't attract a lot of attention from the outside." He stepped into the pretty lake. "Come on."

I raised my brows. "What do you mean?"

"Don't tell me you're scared."

I looked into his teasing eyes. "Maybe."

"Don't worry, I'll be right here." He tossed his shirt aside and dove in.

He swam down through the deep pool-like water and slowly came back up. Surfacing, he slung his head from side to side, sending droplets of water spraying off him.

"You coming?" he asked.

I stripped my shirt over my head, slipped out of my capris, and in my practical bikini (not the string one) I stepped into the warm water.

"Come on." He ducked under.

We swam for a while, enjoying the comfortable warmth of the underground lake, diving down and coming back up. I felt like a mermaid swimming through the water, losing myself in the experience.

I opened my eyes underwater at some point, delighted at being able to see. Beneath the surface, I turned to see Cade watching me, smiling. He waved and I let out a gurgly laugh.

Cade motioned to surface and I followed him up. He motioned to the center of the lake where the sandy island was. "Let's head out there."

I nodded. "Sounds good."

Side by side we swam to the island. Beneath the surface I studied the gradual building of the island, rock upon rock, then sand. When it was shallow enough, we stood and walked the rest of the way.

Wiping the water from my eyes, I glanced over to Cade. "I'm so glad I got in."

He cut me a sideways look. "I knew you would be."

We stepped from the water and Cade flopped onto his back in the sand. He closed his eyes and let out a long breath. "I'm starving."

"Me too." I stretched out beside him and closed my eyes too.

"I've got tons of stuff back at the van," he said.

"Lot of good that does us here."

Cade laughed. "True." He reached over and took my hand.

We lay next to each other, our fingers linked, our eyes closed. My thoughts drifted. I thought about my life before this place, and about my mom and my dad and grandmother. It seemed so far away—and I felt like such a different person. It was amazing how much difference a few weeks could make. I thought of my aunt and the summer. Of all the people I'd met, of Cade. I thought of this day and the swimming and lying here in the sand.

I felt . . . peaceful and completely at ease. There was no other place in the whole world I'd rather have been than right there, right then. And no other person I'd rather have been with than Cade.

"What's the best memory of your whole life?" he softly asked.

I smiled a little at the unexpected, sweet question. "I think this memory right here might qualify."

"And before now?" he asked.

With my eyes still closed, I dug around in my brain, going back as far as I could go. "I'd have to say it goes back to when I was five, or maybe six. I was cuddled up in a big chair with my dad. There was a fire going and he was stroking my hair, reading me a book." I smiled as I recalled the memory.

"Why is that your favorite?" Cade mumbled.

I thought about that for a second. "I guess because it was one of the rare moments in my life when my dad wasn't being formal with me. He was just being a dad." And I'd wished for that again many times over the years.

"And you?" I asked Cade. "What's your favorite memory?"

He didn't answer at first.

I opened my eyes and turned my head to see him staring at the opening in the cave and the sky way up above.

"It's interesting that your favorite memory involves your dad," Cade murmured.

"Why's that?" I whispered.

"Because mine does too."

"Really?"

His answer surprised me. I'd expected his most cherished memory to be of his mom.

"I was around the same age as you—five, maybe six. Sid and I went fishing in a tiny little rowboat. We anchored on the other end of the island in a cove. We did nothing more than sit all day and fish, talk"—Cade chuckled—"get sunburned. We didn't catch anything, got home that night hungry, thirsty. Mom lit into us both about the sunburns. And Sid and I just laughed. . . ."

Cade's voice trailed off and my heart picked up pace. "Why is that your favorite?" I repeated the same question he'd asked me.

Cade swallowed. "Because it's one of the rare memories I have of Sid being a real dad."

I rolled over onto my elbow and looked down at him. "I'm so sorry." I reached over and stroked some wet hairs from his forehead.

He closed his eyes and I continued stroking his hair, staring down at his too-handsome face. And the more I stared, the more I knew I was about to kiss him.

I shifted my body closer and moved my lips softly over his.

Cade returned the kiss, wrapping his arms around me, holding me tight. He repositioned us, rolling me to my back, his body half on, half off of me. He deepened the kiss slowly, taking his time.

Cade shifted, redirecting my thoughts, and nibbled a soft path along my neck. I ran my hands down his back, feeling the hard lines of his muscles.

He moved down a little and pressed a few feathery kisses on my collarbone. I felt his hands along my sides. He moved back up, rubbed his nose affectionately against mine, and then slowly got to his feet.

He held out his hand. "Come on; let's head back."

I took his hand, and Cade walked me back into the water. Together we swam across the underground lake back to the shore. We got out and made our way over to our clothes.

"Just wait until you see what I've got to eat," he told me, slipping his T-shirt back on.

I smiled, absolutely loving the date, loving being with him.

Linking fingers, we made our way through the dark tunnel and back outside. I followed him across the small beach to where we'd left our shoes tied to the bush. He retrieved his and gave me mine.

"Are we eating here, or . . . ?"

"You'll see," he teased, and led the way back up the trail to the van.

We climbed in; he started the engine and pulled away. He took my hand as he drove along the coastal highway to our next destination.

All I could do was breathe in the moist air, smile at the romance, bask in the feeling of our hands together, and adore the beautiful ocean.

Some time later he pulled over to the side of the road and cut the engine. We climbed out of the van. Cade opened the side door and jumped into the cargo area.

He motioned for me to turn around. "Don't watch. I want this to be a surprise."

Smiling, I turned my back to the van and stared out at the Atlantic. Behind me I heard him rustling around. While I listened to him and took in the horizon, I thought about everything we'd said. I had so little time left, and my mind spun with what might happen between us. I felt like we'd wasted such precious dating time.

I sighed, wishing I could do the past weeks over again. There were so many things I would have done differently.

"Ready," Cade said from behind me.

I turned around and sucked in a breath.

A colorful blanket was spread over the floor of the cargo area. In the center Cade had placed a hand-tied bouquet of wildflowers, similar to the one he'd given me on brunch day. On one corner of the blanket he'd set the cooler. And on another corner he had a small stereo.

He reached over and pressed the Play button. Soft music filtered out. Smiling, he held his hand out to me. "Let's chow."

I laughed and, kicking my shoes off, took his hand and climbed into our private picnic place.

"I've put together a very nutritious meal for our culinary pleasure." Cade opened the cooler.

I peeked inside, and I couldn't help myself, I busted out laughing. "Nutritious indeed."

"Cheese curls." He pulled out a giant bag. "Cream puffs." He tossed that to me. "Soda. Honey nuts. Chips. Cookies." On and on he pulled out junk food and placed it in a huge pile.

In front of us, the ocean stretched for eternity. Around us reggae music floated through the air. In our drying clothes and still-damp hair, we ate junk food and talked.

At some point we finished and went for a long walk in the sand. We picked up shells, laughed, and talked. Before I knew it, the sun was going down and we went back to the van. We lay side by side, stretched out on the blanket. When the sun dropped completely below the horizon, we let the moon illuminate us.

On the coastal highway behind us, we heard a few cars pass by. Cade and I lapsed into silence, staring at the moonlit ocean.

A cool breeze blew in off the water and Cade moved closer to keep me warm. We cuddled awhile, still saying nothing, just enjoying.

I don't know what made me—his smell, his warmth, the whole day—but I leaned over and kissed him just as deeply as he'd kissed me in the cave.

Chapter Nineteen

All through breakfast service the next morning, I was completely distracted. I couldn't concentrate on anything. All I could think about was my day with Cade.

I was dying to talk to Gwenny about everything. Finally, after cleaning up the kitchen, I ran up to my room, closed the door, and sat down on my bed with my cell phone. As if she'd read my thoughts, Gwenny texted me at that exact moment.

WELL, HOW'D THE DATE GO?!

AMAZING.

SIGH. KISSING?

YES.

MORE THAN KISSING?

I smiled. I DON'T KISS AND TELL.

TO ME YOU DO!!!!!!!!!!!!

I laughed as a message popped up indicating my grand-mother was calling.

LOL, GMOTHER'S CALLING. TEXT YOU LATER.

I clicked over. "Good morning, Grandmother."

"Elizabeth Margaret, how are you?"

I rolled my eyes at the formality, which seemed so jarring to me now. "I'm fine. Thank you for asking."

Grandmother launched into a whole one-sided conversation, talking about my first week back and telling me that Mom had bought me several new outfits for my internship. I tried to pay attention, but my thoughts kept drifting to Cade and our incredible day.

"Did you hear me?" Grandmother asked.

"Sorry. I'm a bit distracted right now," I honestly answered.

"It's not often I call, and when I do I expect the utmost attention."

I rolled my eyes again. "Yes, ma'am."

She continued on and I listened for a few seconds before my mind began to wander again.

"Elizabeth Margaret, I am absolutely appalled with your lack of focus," my grandmother interrupted my thoughts. "What exactly is so important that you can't spare me a few minutes of conversation time?"

She was right. I *was* being rude. "Sorry—"

"Do you know who you remind me of right now?" Grandmother snapped. "Matilda. She never listened to me."

"Well, maybe she had more important things to think about."

Silence.

I couldn't believe I'd just voiced my thought out loud. It felt . . . liberating.

"Elizabeth Margaret, never have you been so rude. Three weeks with your aunt Matilda has turned you into one very disrespectful young woman."

Three weeks with my aunt Tilly had opened my world to who I really am, I wanted to say, but I didn't dare.

"Matilda's told you, hasn't she?" Grandmother demanded.

My heart picked up pace. "Told me what?"

Silence.

"Told me what?" I asked again, with more urgency.

"Never mind," my grandmother finally said. "Elizabeth Margaret, I have things to do. Good-bye."

She clicked off and I stood at my bedroom window looking at the gorgeous red flowers growing across my glass, completely confused.

"Hey, beautiful." Cade stuck his head inside my open door.

I turned around. "What do you know about Aunt Tilly and my family back in New England?"

Slowly, the smile he'd had for me faded away. "I . . . I don't know anything, Em. I know Tilly didn't get along with her mom and left home at a young age. I know she found her way here and became a maid." Cade shrugged. "That's all."

I sighed and turned back to the window.

"Why don't you just ask Tilly?"

"I did. She won't tell me anything."

Cade crossed the room to where I stood. He put his arms around me and pulled me back against him. "It's not about you, you know. It's about them. They're allowed their secrets."

I hadn't thought about it that way, but Cade was right. Their feud wasn't about me. It was really none of my business. I just happened to be stuck in the middle.

"Hey, guys," Frederick said, stepping into my bedroom.

Cade and I both turned around.

"Oh." Frederick's gaze went between us. "You're hugging," he said, stating the obvious. "So are you two a thing now?"

Cade looked at me. "Yep, I guess you could say that." He planted a quick kiss on my lips, then crossed my room and headed out the door. On a side note, he turned back. "Hey, come find me later. I want to show you something."

I smiled. "OK."

Cade continued on, and I busied myself making my bed.

After a few seconds, I realized Frederick hadn't moved and glanced over my shoulder to see him staring at me.

I lifted my brows. "What's up?"

He sighed. "You're going to be leaving soon."

I sighed too. "I know. Bummer, huh?"

Frederick nodded. "Major bummer. Too bad you can't just stay."

My shoulders dropped. "I know." Staying *would* be incredible. Even though I had been there only a short while, I felt as though I really belonged. It was hard to imagine going back to my old life. "It's OK." I crossed the short distance between us and wrapped my arms around him. "We'll definitely keep in touch."

He squeezed me back.

Aunt Tilly walked into my room. "Well, it's a family affair

in here." She stopped when she saw us, and a smile quirked her lips. "Am I interrupting?"

We pulled apart. "Just a little bonding," I said, keeping one arm looped around Frederick's waist.

Aunt Tilly looked between us. "You two are something else."

Frederick and I exchanged a glance.

Tilly put a basket of laundry down on my bed. "I'd hoped that you two would hit it off, but I can see you've done more than that. You have no idea how happy that makes me."

Frederick and I exchanged another glance. And to think I had no clue I had a cousin until arriving at the Pepper House. Now I couldn't imagine *not* having him in my life.

"Anyway . . ." Aunt Tilly fluttered her fingers. "Harry said to tell you the waffles were excellent this morning."

"Harry . . . ? Oh." I suddenly remembered. "Harold, the yacht man. Who is he, by the way? His name sounds familiar."

Aunt Tilly shrugged. "No idea." She turned to Frederick. "Mind running a few errands for me?"

"Sure."

The two of them left and I went to look for Cade.

* * *

I found Cade out in front of the Pepper House, under the hood of the van. "So, um"—I leaned up against the van—"Frederick's going to miss me when I leave."

Cade kept his head under the hood. "So, um," he said, mimicking me, "I am too."

I smiled. "How much?"

Cade brought his head out. "Looking for a boost to your ego?"

I laughed.

He came out from under the hood. "You better be careful or I'll smear grease on you." He held his dirty fingers up and wiggled them menacingly.

I giggled, and the sound made me giggle some more. I couldn't ever recall having *giggled*. Giggling was for brainless girls. And that thought made me giggle some more. *Giggling was for brainless girls.* That sounded like my mom.

Grinning, Cade backed me up against the truck. "Well, look at you giggling."

I slapped his arm. "I'm *not* giggling." And then I giggled some more.

Cade leaned in to nuzzle his nose in my neck. "Yes, you *are* giggling. And"—he kissed my skin—"you smell terrific."

Laughing, I pushed him away. "You're getting me dirty."

"Dirty? Here, I can fix that," he said, reaching toward me. "Come here."

I batted his hand away. "Stop!" I laughed even harder.

He got this exaggerated, concentrated look on his face and grabbed my chin with one hand. He pretended to lick his thumb and proceeded to scrub away dirt from my cheek.

"Gross!" I pushed him away.

Laughing, he wiped his dirty hands on a rag and took my hand. "Come on. I want to show you something."

He led me inside. "I'm going to get my box from your bedroom," he told my aunt as we passed through the living room.

She smiled knowingly. "OK."

"Box?" I asked. "What box?"

He gave my hand a little tug. "You'll see."

I followed Cade through the kitchen and up the back stairs. He led me into Aunt Tilly's room and over to her closet. I watched as he pushed her clothes aside, scooting some shoes out of the way and sliding a midsized cardboard box free.

He sat down on the floor and pulled the box over in front of him. As he pried the flaps open, I knelt down across from him.

Carefully, Cade reached in and pulled out a small tissue-wrapped object. He cradled it in his hands and gently unwrapped it.

A tiny pink-and-white glass fairy stared back at me, her face curved into a mischievous smile. Pale pink wings extended out of her back and dark pink hair flowed down the length of her body.

I looked up at Cade. "She's beautiful."

"My mom made her."

My eyes widened and I looked back down at the fairy. "She's so delicate . . . and little." She couldn't have been more than two inches in length.

He handed her to me, and I very, *very* gently held her in my palms. "I can't believe your mom made this." The small fairy was so fragile, as if the slightest movement of my fingers could snap her in half. It made me nervous to hold her.

Cade reached into the box and pulled out another object, this one a bit bigger. Just as carefully he peeled the wrapping away to reveal a blue glass dragon. About double the size of the fairy, the glass dragon was just as detailed. Varying hues of blue defined its features, its body, its tail, and it had fire coming from its mouth.

He put the dragon down and reached in to pull out another object. And then another, and then another. One by one he unwrapped each, taking just as much time and care. The blown-glass pieces ranged in size from ten inches down to the tiny two-inch fairy. And his mom had used every color imaginable.

A wizard, a witch, the dragon, the fairy, a prince, a princess . . . "Seems as if your mom liked fairy tales," I observed.

Cade smiled. "She loved them."

When he finished with the last, a unicorn, and set it next to all the rest, I looked over at him. Smiling, he touched each one, running his finger along the smooth glass. The love I saw on his face touched me to my very core.

I was sure his mom occupied every corner of his mind right at that moment. I wanted to ask him what particular memory he was thinking of. Instead, I handed the fairy back to him. "Thank you for sharing these with me."

Cade glanced over at me and smiled. "You're very welcome." And then he leaned across the small distance and gave me a tender kiss.

He pulled back. "Any interest in seeing some pictures of her?"

I smiled. "Definitely."

He nodded toward the closet. "Blue-and-white box." He started rewrapping the blown glass figurines. "Mind getting it?"

"Sure." I headed across the floor and into my aunt's closet. I parted her long clothes and peered over her shoes into the back. There was only one blue-and-white box, and so I assumed that was the one. I glanced around the closet for the "Family Pics" album I had discovered on my first morning at the Pepper House, but I didn't see it. Grabbing the box, I lifted it out and made my way back over to Cade.

I helped him rewrap the last of the figurines and we carefully repacked the box. I wondered what I would keep and cherish of my mother's if she died. Her fancy furniture? Her expensive silverware? Her designer clothes? I couldn't think of anything I'd treasure the way Cade did his mom's glass art. The realization made me very sad.

Now, Aunt Tilly, I could think of a handful of things I'd hold close to my heart: the plumed pen she used in her office, the thin bracelets she always wore, the ivory comb that sat on her dresser . . .

I could think of lots more, and I'd only known her for less than a month. It was strange to think of how much closer to her I felt than to my own mother.

Cade grabbed the blue-and-white box and pulled the lid off. Inside were photos. Some black-and-white, others color. Small ones, big ones. The majority were worn around the edges.

He reached inside and brought out a handful. He showed me one of a blond-haired woman hugging a small boy. With matching grins they cheesed it for the camera. "Me and my mom," Cade said, handing me the picture.

I studied the photo of the young woman with the windblown hair and a very cute little Cade. I recognized the backdrop as the front of the Pepper House. "She's very pretty."

He smiled. "Thanks." He handed me another one. "The three of us."

In this one, Sid, Cade, and his mom cuddled together on what I recognized as Sid's sailboat. They looked like they were a family in love. Cade couldn't have been more than two. And Sid looked so . . . different. Younger. Healthier. Happier.

"That was right before Sid did one of his famous disappearing acts," Cade said. "He took his boat out and just didn't come back for a month."

"I'm sorry, Cade." I didn't know what else to say.

He shrugged and handed me another photo, making it clear he really didn't want to expound on things.

He kept showing me pictures, mostly of him and his mom. Snapshots taken all over the island. A few had Aunt Tilly in them and a dark-haired man I assumed was Roger Pepper. There were some with Sid, but very few. It made me sad for the childhood Cade hadn't had with his father.

He gave me one last photo to look at before getting up. "Be right back."

Nodding, I watched him leave Aunt Tilly's room. A few seconds later I heard his footsteps on the stairs as he trotted down to the main floor. I gave the picture a quick glance to see a grinning Cade holding a conch shell. I'd say he was probably five or six years old.

Smiling at his sweet, innocent face, I began organizing the photos, neatly putting them into stacks.

I glanced up again to where I had found the family photo album and remembered the photos I had seen. Remembered how protective my aunt had gotten over the book. Remembered Frederick saying there were other albums .

Kneeling, I started moving things around in her closet. I was being nosy. I knew that. But I couldn't help myself.

Under a blanket I saw several worn albums and pulled them all out. Quickly, I thumbed through one with mostly pictures of Frederick. I leafed through another, this one with scenic shots of travel. I opened the last and saw a black-and-white photo of a young Tilly with my mom. My heart skipped as I turned the page and saw a very old photo of my grandmother and grandfather.

I flipped another page to a photo of a young-looking Tilly sitting propped up in a hospital bed holding a tiny infant. Frederick, maybe? With a tear-streaked face she tried her best to smile for the camera, but anyone could tell they weren't tears of joy. Had her delivery of Frederick been hard on her?

I looked at the date stamped in the bottom corner and did a quick calculation to seventeen, almost eighteen years ago. There was no way that baby could be fifteen-year-old Frederick. I looked at the date stamp again and realized it was my birthday.

"Em?"

I glanced over my shoulder to see Aunt Tilly standing in the doorway. "Cade said you two were looking through his family pictures?"

I held the album up. "Is this you?" I looked at it again. Maybe the young girl was my mom and I just thought it was Aunt Tilly. They did look a lot alike.

She didn't answer me at first and instead just stood there staring at me.

"Aunt Tilly?"

She swallowed. "Yes. Yes, it's me."

"Well, then . . ." I studied the photo, completely and utterly confused. "Who is this baby?"

Aunt Tilly took a deep breath and let it out slowly.

"Tilly?"

"It's . . . um . . . it's you," she softly replied.

I looked back at the photo and zeroed in on the baby. "But . . . why are you in a hospital gown?"

Her eyes teared up. "Because . . . Em"—she cleared her throat—"that's . . . that's the day I delivered you."

I stared at her, mute, processing what she'd said and at the same time unable to wrap my brain around it.

The day she delivered me?

I glanced back down at the picture, gradually becoming aware of my body—sort of numb, kind of floating. Something in my ears rang, the room began to blur, and I squeezed my eyes shut.

The day she delivered me?

I focused on my heart, now thudding hard in my chest, and realized I wasn't breathing. I inhaled, exhaled, and opened my eyes.

Behind Aunt Tilly, Cade reentered the bedroom. "Did ya miss m—" His voice cut away as he looked to me, Aunt Tilly, and back to me. "What's going on?"

"The day . . ." I paused. "You deliv—" I swallowed. "Me?"

Aunt Tilly swallowed too. "Yes."

I swung my gaze to Cade and held up the album. "Did you know about this?" Somewhere in the back of my mind I knew that it really didn't matter just then, but it was all I could think to say.

Cade looked between Tilly and me. "Um . . ."

Aunt Tilly glanced over her shoulder to where he stood. "Can you give us some time?"

Cade brought his gaze back to me and, with a slight nod, quietly closed the door.

Aunt Tilly turned to me. "I was sixteen when I got pregnant. Seventeen when I had you. I was scared. It was an accident. I convinced myself that the boy who got me pregnant loved me. I thought we were going to get married or live together or something. I thought we were going to raise you together. But your grandmother was so angry, so ashamed, she kicked me out of the house. I had nowhere to go. I was living with the boy for a while, but a week before I gave birth he left, and I never heard from him again."

I tried to listen to what she was saying, but I couldn't quite focus. I had nothing to hold on to, emotionally or physically, but the photo album.

Aunt Tilly's entire face seemed to be frowning in pain and I got the distinct impression she was trying to say everything as quickly as possible. Trying to purge her soul. "I went back to your grandmother, begged her to let me stay until you were born. I promised I would leave right after." She paused, took a breath. "My older sister, your mom, had everything. The husband, the house, the stability—the perfect life. She wanted children, but they were having trouble conceiving. Of course later Gwyneth, your sister, showed up unexpectedly."

Your mom, I latched on to that phrase. My mom wasn't really my mom. This woman in front of me, my aunt Tilly, was really *my mom*.

"I didn't know how I'd provide for you. Where I'd live. Your grandmother told me the state would take you away from me because of my situation. I was young. I didn't know. But she was probably right anyway. I wasn't fit to mother you." Aunt Tilly reached out to me. "Please don't think ill of your grandmother. She was only acting out of love."

I knew my grandmother. She rarely did anything out of love. Especially not if it might tarnish her image.

"She told me," Aunt Tilly railroaded on, "if I gave you to Katherine, your mom, she'd raise you like her own. No one would know. You'd have the best of everything—more than I could have or ever would have been able to give." Aunt Tilly took a deep breath. "I was defiant. Thought I could do it anyway. But the day you were born and I held you in my arms . . . I knew I had to. I didn't want anything to happen to you. And as hard as it was, I knew that giving you up was the best thing for you."

Somewhere in the back of my mind I knew my ears had stopped ringing, my body wasn't numb, my heart wasn't racing, and I was completely, utterly focused on her every word.

"Your grandmother had her lawyers draw up the paperwork. The agreement was that if I signed custody over to Katherine, they'd raise you with the best of everything, and I would never show my face again. Your grandmother told me she'd send me anywhere I wanted to go—one-way ticket. I picked the Outer Banks because it happened to be on the news that day. Soon after, Katherine got a job at the hospital; your dad had just been promoted. You, your parents, and grandmother moved on and no one knew differently."

Aunt Tilly stopped talking then, and the first thing to pop into my head was, "Were you ever going to tell me?"

"I don't know, Em. God knows I wanted to. But . . . I just didn't know. I didn't know what kind of person you were. How you'd handle it. If we'd hit it off." She shook her head. "There are a lot of things involved with something so huge. And I'd promised your grandmother and mother I wouldn't. That was the only way they'd let you come visit me."

A million questions bounced around in my brain, but I couldn't pick one to ask first.

Tilly sucked in a breath. "Em—"

I looked at her, and before I could figure out what I was feeling or ask one single question, she began crying uncontrollably and fled from the room.

Chapter Twenty

I didn't know how long I sat there on Aunt Tilly's bedroom floor. I didn't remember getting up and walking downstairs, or leaving the Pepper House. I must have made my way to the beach because by the time I realized where I was, it was dusk and I was walking along the shoreline.

Hours passed in a sort of daze as I thought and rethought conversations Aunt Tilly and I had had. All the cryptic statements and questions that she, my mom, and grandmother had said to me.

Has . . . Matilda told you anything about our family? Mom asked.

When I was sixteen, I got in trouble, Aunt Tilly admitted.

Matilda's told you, hasn't she? Grandmother demanded.

And to think I'd thought their quarrel had nothing to do

with me. It had *everything* to do with me. *I* was the reason behind their feud.

With a sigh, I glanced up and realized I was at the beach where Cade and I had surfed. I sat down next to a sand dune and picked a sea oat from the ground. I tried to put myself in Aunt Tilly's place—young, pregnant, being threatened by Grandmother, being dumped by the father of my child. I couldn't even imagine. And then more of Aunt Tilly's words floated through my mind . . .

I never did like living in your grandmother's house. Too many rules. Too much formality. Too much everything. I was always rebellious, sneaking out, purposefully doing things to make her angry. I look back on that now and am certainly not proud of my behavior.

Purposefully doing things to make Grandmother angry? Did Aunt Tilly get pregnant on purpose? I couldn't imagine that, but maybe I didn't know Aunt Tilly after all.

When I was sixteen, I got in trouble. So she considered me trouble? I thought pregnancies were supposed to be blessings.

Blessings? Please. If I got pregnant right now, I thought, I certainly wouldn't think of it as a blessing. I'd be freaked out. Blessings were for older couples, married, maybe had been trying for a while, and then voilà. Pregnant.

Right? So I guessed that would make my sister a blessing to my parents. And me? Something they *had* to take on because of Grandmother's request. Because they couldn't have children and thought raising me would be their last hope.

Well, lucky for them my sister came along, because I

certainly didn't turn out to be the perfect daughter they'd wanted.

I shut my eyes, more than irritated with myself and the direction my thoughts were heading. The last thing I needed was to pick apart my insecurities. The fact was, as daughters went, I was a pretty darn good one. And I was sick and tired of not only doubting that, but trying to prove it.

I opened my eyes and took a deep breath. Now I just needed to figure out how to handle all this new information in my life.

"Em?"

I glanced up. Cade stood a careful distance away, clearly not sure if he should approach. I smiled a little and he took that as his cue to come closer. He sat down behind me and pulled me into his arms.

I didn't know what it was . . . His smell. His warmth. My tired brain. My spinning thoughts that had just slowed. Hours on an emotional roller coaster. I didn't know what it was . . . but tears welled up and flowed over and I didn't stop them. I cried about my life, Aunt Tilly, memories, the situation, my family back in New England, what I was going to do, what I *wasn't* going to do . . . I cried tears that I felt had been in me for a while. Uncontrollable tears, and I freely let them come.

Cade didn't say anything, just held me.

Some time later, the tears slowed and eventually stopped. I sniffled and wiped my eyes with my shirt. Cade dug a couple of napkins from his pocket and handed them to me.

I didn't care how I looked—red eyes, snotty nose, and all. I turned and curled into Cade's chest and he continued holding me, caressing my hair.

I closed my eyes and concentrated on his even breathing. Once I felt calm enough, I opened my mouth, took a deep breath of my own, and told him everything. He listened quietly, knowing, I suspected, that was exactly what I needed. I didn't want advice, just someone with an open ear.

We stayed that way, him holding me, lapsing into silence. I might have fallen asleep. I didn't know how much time had passed when Cade finally got up and pulled me to my feet. Holding my hand, he led me from the beach and out onto the road where his moped sat. We rode back into town and to Cade's apartment.

Chapter Twenty-one

I awoke the next morning snuggled in Cade's futon bed. I opened one eye to find Cade, waving a sugary doughnut back and forth in front of my face. A lemon-glazed doughnut to be exact. Reaching one hand out of the blankets, I snatched it away and took a big bite, and then another. I didn't think a doughnut had ever tasted so good.

He produced coffee next.

I sat up and took that, too. "You're pretty handy to have around." I enjoyed a sweet sip of white-chocolate mocha.

Giving me one of his sexy half-smiles, he leaned down and delivered a quick kiss to my lips. "Are you going to be OK? I've gotta go to work." He stood. "See you there?"

I took another sip, pondering that question. By work he meant the Pepper House. "Um . . ." I really didn't think I was ready to face Tilly yet. And my . . . *brother*. That was right. Frederick *was* my brother, not my cousin.

"On second thought, why don't you hang out here," Cade volunteered, saving me from making a decision. "I'll let everyone know where you are."

I smiled through a sigh. "Thanks. That sounds good."

Cade blew me a kiss and was gone.

I sat there for a few minutes, listening to the quiet, sipping my coffee.

Slowly, everything came back to me—what Tilly told me the night before, how everything was now different. Then it hit me—I'd never know who my father was. Gwenny wasn't my sister; she was my cousin. Everything I'd ever believed to be true, wasn't. It was all so overwhelming. What were my first words to Aunt Tilly going to be? *Hi, Mom?*

No, that didn't sound right.

Where do we go from here?

Where *did* we go from here? Did I start calling her Mom? Did I tell my mom back home that I knew the family secret? Did I tell my sister? Did I tell *Frederick?*

I let out a breath, realizing my brain was spinning with too many questions. I'd been through that already. I couldn't bear to go through it again.

I threw the covers aside and padded into Cade's bathroom. Using his guy stuff, I showered and shampooed, and emerged smelling like the woods.

I rifled through Cade's closet and found a T-shirt and board shorts that almost fit me.

I nosed around in his kitchen, pleased to find it not as barren as I'd imagined. I scrambled up some eggs and brewed some more coffee. I stripped the sheets off the mattress and folded the futon back into a sofa. I swept his hardwood floor. I dusted. I wiped down his counters. I did a once-over in his bathroom. Then I began studying his living area. A bouquet of flowers there, a tall light here, move the couch there . . .

With a sigh, I looked at the cleaning rag in my hand. I was wasting time, avoiding reality. I had no business hiding out in his place. I needed to go see Aunt Tilly. But more important, I needed to face my mom and grandmother and figure all this out.

I turned to get ready, and the door opened and Cade walked in.

I looked up from where I stood, holding the rag. "Hi."

Cade closed his front door and looked around his apartment. "You cleaned."

I nodded.

He sniffed. "And cooked."

"Eggs. Coffee."

"Any left?"

I shook my head. "Didn't know you'd be back so soon."

He gave me a once-over. "You look cute in my clothes."

I looked down at myself. "Thanks. You don't mind . . . ?"

He shook his head.

"Go OK at the Pepper House?"

Cade nodded. "Tilly said to take as much time as you needed. She was just glad to know you're safe."

I smiled. Aunt Tilly knew I needed time. Tilly knew I was safe with Cade. My real mom *knew* me. My mother, on the other hand, would have launched an all-out search party for me.

But, I realized, that was because she loved me too . . . she just had a different way of showing it.

Cade came toward me. "I came back because I was worried about you."

"Cade . . ."

"And," he said, clearing his throat, "I need to tell you something."

A knock sounded on his door, and Cade sighed.

"Can we talk later?" I asked.

He nodded and went to see who was at the door. Frederick stood on the other side. He looked right across the apartment at me.

"Hey," I quietly greeted him.

Cade motioned Frederick inside. "I'll leave you two alone," he said, and closed the door behind him.

Frederick just stood there, kind of slump-shouldered, looking at the floor. I stood across the apartment looking at him.

Neither of us spoke for a few long seconds.

I interrupted the silence. "You know?"

He nodded, slowly bringing his eyes up to meet mine. "Mom told me last night."

"So . . . so what do you think about the whole thing?"

"I was really upset."

My heart sank. "Oh."

"I mean, to think of what this all means. That you're my real sister. I . . ." He shrugged. "I don't know. It's just really . . . confusing."

I didn't want Frederick mad at me or at Aunt Tilly. This whole thing affected him on a completely different level, and he needed time to process it too.

"Don't get me wrong," he went on, "I think it's pretty cool we're brother and sister."

I smiled a little. "I think it's pretty cool too." Actually, *very* cool. Frederick was about as great as they came.

"Mom and I have always been straight-up about things. So I can't believe she hid this from me."

I moved a little closer to my brother, truly feeling his confusion. "Guess this explains all the secrecy in our family."

He let out a humorless laugh. "Guess so."

"Don't blame Tilly. She was so young. Younger than me, even," I realized. "Scared."

Frederick nodded. "I know. I guess . . . I guess I just wanted to talk to you."

"I wanted to talk to you, too."

He sighed. "Well, and there it is."

"Yeah, there it is." I closed the distance between us and gave him a hug. "I can't think of a better brother to have."

He squeezed me back. "Same here. Sister, that is."

We shared a chuckle.

I took a step back. "You here on a moped?"

He nodded.

"Double me back? I think it's time I talked to Tilly."

Cade walked back into the apartment as I was writing him a quick note. "I'm glad you're still here. I have to tell you two something."

We turned toward the door, both surprised to see him back again.

He let out a breath and looked between us.

"Cade?" I prompted.

"I'm just going to say it, so—"

"Say what?" I interrupted.

"I knew," he hurriedly admitted. "I've known for years."

Frederick and I just looked at him, confused, his words slowly sinking in.

"What?" Frederick whispered.

"I knew," Cade said again. He shook his head with regret and swallowed. "I'm sorry. I found out by accident. I overheard Tilly and Domino talking one night and—"

I just stood there, staring. I couldn't believe what I was hearing. *Cade knew?*

Shaking his head, Frederick brushed past him. "I can't deal with this right now," he snapped at Cade. He glanced over his shoulder at me as he headed out the door. "Coming?"

Irritation and betrayal slowly took form as I looked at the guilt on Cade's face. "You should have said something," I told him, and followed Frederick out.

Chapter Twenty-two

As Frederick and I rode back to the Pepper House, I tried very hard not to think of Cade. Frankly, I didn't know what *to* think of him.

I blocked him from my brain so I could focus on what I was going to say to Tilly. I would walk in, see her, and go with it from there.

We pulled into the front and Frederick cut the engine. "You nervous?"

I let out a breath. "I'm trying not to be."

"Want me to come with you?"

"No, that's OK." I got off the moped.

"I'm going to drive around a bit," he told me, "and just think about stuff."

I nodded. "Want to talk about Cade?"

Frederick shook his head. "I don't know what to say. I'm so aggravated right now. I just need a little time."

I nodded again and watched him putter off. I didn't know what to say either. It seemed like everyone around here had been hiding things from me. Everyone except Frederick.

I . . . I don't know anything, Em. I know Tilly didn't get along with her mom and left home at a young age. I know she found her way here and became a maid.

With a sigh, I shook Cade's lying words from my head and turned toward the Pepper House. "Focus—one thing at a time," I mumbled to myself.

A few seconds passed. As I stared at the front door, I thought about everything that had happened in the short time I'd been there. I'd been lied to by Tilly. Betrayed by Cade. I treated Jeremy horribly and failed at wowing Domino with my first brunch attempt—yet I still convinced myself I wanted to go against everything my parents wanted and be a chef.

I shook my head. None of this seemed like me. Maybe coming to the Outer Banks hadn't been such a great idea.

But as I continued staring at the front door, the one word that kept circling in my brain was "home."

With another deep sigh, I let myself into the Pepper House.

Home. It hit me again as I took in the hardwood floors, the driftwood furniture, the tropical plants, and the warm glow from the corner lamp.

A couple of older women sat across from each other playing chess. I immediately thought of Frederick and the numerous games we'd played. *Home.*

I made my way through the great room and into the dining room. The scent of chicken cacciatore lingered in the air.

Through the windows that bordered the dining room, I saw a couple of people sitting by the bay. From the long blond hair I knew Tilly was one of them.

I blew out a calming breath and headed for the back door. The island's warm breeze bathed my body as I quietly walked toward her. When I drew near I recognized the other person with her as Harold Lemley, the man from the yacht.

With his arm stretched along the back of the swing, he sat closely beside my aunt, and together they silently took in the bay. They looked content and very at ease with their friendly companionship. It made me happy.

"Hi," I greeted them.

They both turned.

"Em." Tilly spoke as if she'd been expecting me.

I took a step toward her. "Can we talk?"

Harold stood. "I'll leave you two ladies to things."

As he walked across the yard and disappeared down the cottage's path, I took a seat beside my aunt on the swing. "You know, I've been standing outside for a while, staring at the front door. I thought of the lies, the betrayal, the different ways I've failed this month. It's not what I expected coming here."

"Em—"

"I guess I came here thinking I was going to find myself or something. And I did. I found more than myself."

"Em—"

"But I also can't seem to shake the word 'home' from my mind. This place really does feel like home, Tilly." I sighed. "And I don't know what to do about that."

She reached out and took my hand.

I closed my eyes in relief. I didn't know what I had expected. Coldness? Distance? It was ridiculous, really. She'd never been that way to me before. Why would she start now?

I slid across the swing at the same time she leaned toward me, and we went into each other's arms. She hugged me snug against her as if she hadn't hugged me in years. I returned her cozy embrace, relishing how just plain *good* it felt to be held so tight.

"I love you," she whispered.

Her words brought a flood of tears to my eyes. "I love you, too."

"Oh, Em." Her breath caught on her own tears and she squeezed me even harder.

We sat that way, hugging, crying, for I didn't know how long.

"I don't blame you," I told her as I pulled back a little. "I would have been just as scared. Feeling hopeless and lost if the father of my baby left. Manipulated by Grandmother. Wanting the best for my baby . . ." I sniffed. "I don't blame you."

"Oh, sweet girl." She cupped my cheek in her hand and looked at me through her own wet eyes. "I know it's a lot to take in."

I nodded. "It is."

Her lips trembled. "How do you feel? Are you angry?"

"No." And I truly meant it. "At first, maybe, I was, but only because I hadn't thought it out."

She smoothed her hand over my hair.

"Frederick and I talked," I told her.

She nodded. "He was really upset last night. He hasn't spoken to me today." She glanced out at the bay. "I hope he'll come around."

"He will," I assured her.

We both sat silent for a minute.

"I've really made a mess of things," she murmured.

"Oh, Tilly." I turned to her. "No, you haven't."

"Who knows if I should've done things differently . . . Kept you? Told Frederick earlier? Tried to get you back?" She shrugged. "I've driven myself nuts thinking about it over the years."

"You did what you thought was right," I said, defending her.

She glanced at me with tears in her eyes.

"Did you tell Cade not to say anything when he found out?" I asked.

Tilly sniffed. "Cade?"

I waited for her to go on, but clearly she was confused. "He said he overheard you and Domino talking . . ."

"Oh," she gasped. "I didn't know. He never said anything. How long ago?"

"He said years."

"Years?" Tilly's eyes widened.

I nodded.

"Poor Cade," she sighed, seeming so brokenhearted that it nearly broke my own heart. "I really have made a mess of things."

I put my arms around her again and laid my head on her shoulder. "It's going to be OK. We're all going to be OK."

But as I thought about all the new developments, and about my life back home, something told me it might not be true.

Chapter Twenty-three

I spent the rest of the afternoon thinking of what I was going to say to Mom, Grandmother, and, most important, my sister. By dinnertime I was mentally exhausted, and thankful I was helping Domino in the kitchen to get my mind off of things.

When I walked in, he just nodded and I smiled at him. We didn't speak, just fell into our prepping and cooking rhythm.

After dinner, I went up to my room and called Gwenny.

"Hey!" she answered.

I smiled. "Hey. You have time to talk?"

"Ooh, sounds serious."

"Are you alone? No one can hear?"

She didn't answer right away. "Yeesss . . ." she said hesitantly. "Em, what's going on? Are you OK?"

I took a deep breath and told her everything. From finding the picture of Tilly holding me, to everything Tilly and I had talked about, and Frederick, and spending the night with Cade. I explained all the crazy emotions I'd been through. I told her about Cade knowing, too. When I was done, I asked, "So?"

She didn't speak.

"Gwenny?"

"Em . . ." I heard tears in her voice.

"It's OK, Gwenny. I know it's a lot."

She cried then. "What . . . what are you going to do? What are *we* going to do?"

I loved that she'd said *we*, but I hated the question she had asked. "I'm staying here," I told her, feeling absolutely sure about my decision, but at the same time feeling awful. "I haven't asked Tilly yet, but she did say this was home for me. I know that's the last thing you want to hear, and I'm so, so sorry for that. But I'm sure, Gwenny. I'm really sure it's what I want."

She didn't respond to that.

"Say something," I prompted.

"You're not coming back?" She sniffed. "Have you told Mom and Grandmother that?"

"Not yet."

"They're going to be furious, Em. Just a sec," I heard her put the phone down and blow her nose. She picked the phone back up. "I'm here."

"Oh, Gwenny. I know this is hard for you. It's breaking my heart that you're so upset."

"It's OK," she mumbled. "I'll be OK."

A few silent seconds passed.

"I'm not going to Harvard, either," I continued softly, feeling absolutely sure about that decision as well.

Gwenny let out a watery chuckle. "Jeez, Em, how many other things are you going to hit me with?"

"I'm going to take the semester off and apply to culinary institutions." I didn't know where all this was coming from. I hadn't really thought about any of it, but as I said it, it felt right.

"Oh, Em," Gwenny started to cry again, "that sounds just perfect for you."

Neither of us said anything for a few seconds.

"What about Mom? And Grandmother?" Gwenny asked.

I took a seat on my bed, just then realizing I'd been nervously pacing. "Well, I thought about coming home and seeing them in person. And then I considered a phone call. But now I'm contemplating a letter. What do you think?"

Gwenny sighed. "I'd love to see you. I'd love for you to come home, but I think a letter really is the best way to go. Mom and Grandmother can be very intimidating. They might even disown you like they did Aunt Tilly. Do you really want to go through that drama?"

I hadn't thought about that, but she was right. I *could* see them telling me to leave and never come back. Especially now that I knew what had happened with Tilly. "They aren't exactly the type *not* to hold grudges."

We both got silent again.

"Why don't you write that letter, and let me know when you send it. Once they've had time to digest everything I'll work on them over here. Eventually, we're bound to wear them down."

I smiled. I loved my sister. "I want you to know this doesn't change anything between us," I told her. "We're still sisters and will always be."

"Em," Gwenny said with a hitch in her vocie, "I just got my tears all dried up."

We shared a laugh.

"I love you, Gwenny. We'll talk later."

We hung up, and I had a horrible sense she was going to feel some of the fallout over all of this.

I took a tablet of paper and went downstairs to the kitchen. I wanted to get started on my letter while I had all my thoughts straight in my head. Domino was just packing up food as I entered.

"Hey," he said, eyeing me. This time, there wasn't any prepping to preoccupy us. I knew something had to be said.

"So, you know everything?"

He nodded. "Always have."

I sat down on one of the stools. "And?"

"And I'm glad you're finally here. Tilly has longed for you for as long as I've known her. There were a lot of hard decisions in all this, and she did what she thought best. Honestly."

I nodded. "I know."

He opened the refrigerator. "When you took off yesterday and were gone all night, she was worried sick. She stayed up

all night waiting on you. And with Frederick upset too"—
Domino shook his head—"not a good night for Tilly."

My heart sank. "I . . . I didn't realize. I needed time to
think. I'm . . . I'm sorry."

Domino sighed. "I know you did, and I'm not getting onto
you. I love Tilly like a sister, and it hurts me when she's hurt.
She's an amazing woman. That's all."

"She is," I agreed.

He leaned back against the sink and folded his arms. "Well?
What's in that pretty little head of yours?"

I told him everything I'd just said to Gwenny. About
staying, not going to Harvard, and applying to culinary schools.
I also told him about the letter I planned to write home. "What
do you think?"

He smiled. "Well, I'm happy you've decided to stay. And
I'm not surprised about your plan for culinary school. You
were screaming world-famous chef the evening you tasted my
snapper."

I smiled, remembering.

"As far as the letter home? I'm not one to *not* do things in
person. I like face-to-face conversations. But from what I know
about your mainland family, I think a letter's a great idea."

I tapped my notepad. "I figured writing it in the kitchen,
my favorite place, would keep me calm and focused."

Domino playfully rolled his eyes. "You are so like me, it's
scary. I do all my main thinking in a kitchen." He pushed off
the sink. "OK, I'll leave you to it."

I picked up my pen and started writing.

Dear Family,

*I have had a wonderful summer here with Tilly. I've
discovered a lot about myself and am a different person
now than when I first arrived. I have become a person
that I am comfortable with and that's a wonderful way
to feel.*

*I have been hiding something from you all for a very
long time. Since I was a little girl I have been incredibly
interested in cooking. So much so that I have numerous
books on the culinary arts and I have snuck into the
kitchen many late nights to practice recipes. Cooking just
plain makes me happy. . . .*

I wrote how I knew the truth about Tilly, and how I felt about
it and about her. I wrote about my mom and grandmother,
about the life plan they had for me, and my own desire to be a
chef. It felt like I was writing for hours, but I finally put the pen
down and reread my lines. I had tried very hard to be neutral
and not put blame on anybody throughout the letter. I felt like
I succeeded.

"Em?"

I glanced up to see Frederick standing in the doorway. He
gestured at the letter. "What's up?"

"To my family back home."

"Oh?" He took a hesitant few steps in.

I slid the pad over. "Mind taking a look? I could use a
second set of eyes."

"Sure." He picked the tablet up and quietly perused it.

When he was done, he put the pad down and gave me a hug. "I'm glad you're staying."

I hugged him back, smiling, loving the warmth and tenderness. "Me too."

Frederick sat down beside me. "Em," he said, "Cade's gone."

"What? What do you mean Cade's gone?"

"I went over to his apartment to talk and his neighbor said he's gone."

I felt panic set in. "Did she say where he went?"

He shook his head.

I sighed, my heart aching. I'd been mad at Cade, but not so mad that I wanted him to leave.

Frederick dropped his head. "Do you think we were too hard on him?"

Before I could answer, Beth swung through the kitchen door. "Will you all *please* tell me what's going on?"

Frederick and I looked at each other.

"Cade's disappeared. You and Tilly are arguing," she said, pointing at Frederick, "And you," she said, jabbing her finger at me, "didn't even sleep here last night. Oh, and Domino's not talking either." She threw her hands up. "Someone tell me *what* is going on."

Frederick and I exchanged another look and then we both began talking at once. We told her everything.

When we were done, Beth just looked at us. Then she slowly slid onto the stool beside me. "Wow."

I suppose that was all she could think to say. I knew the feeling.

She let out a breath. "That's a lot to take in."

I glanced at Frederick. "Tell us about it."

A few quiet seconds passed as Beth mulled everything over. "I'm adopted," she very unexpectedly announced.

I blinked. "You are?"

She nodded. "It's how I ended up here, actually. My parents told me on my eighteenth birthday, and I was so upset I ran away from home." Beth chuckled. "I've never told anyone that before now. They all think I came here for a boy."

Frederick and I shared a surprised look.

With a sigh, Beth looked at me. "My biggest regret is that I didn't talk to my parents for a whole year. I totally froze them out. And I'm not proud of that at all. They're fantastic people and I was horrible to them after they adopted and raised me."

"Did you find your birth parents?" Frederick asked.

Beth shrugged. "I looked for my birth mother for a couple of years, but in the end I gave up. I realized it doesn't matter. It wasn't going to change my life, or who I was."

Beth and I had more in common than I ever imagined.

"My advice to you two? Don't be angry. There's too much love in this home for that."

Frederick and I both smiled. Beth was right. And we needed to find Cade and make sure he knew it too.

Chapter Twenty-four

I went back to Cade's apartment and talked to his neighbor. He had left me a note, brief, saying he had to go away for a while. With nothing left to do, and no way to track him down, I went back to the Pepper House.

Domino and I spent the next few days researching culinary schools. I filled out an application to each of my top five choices: one in Italy, another in France, the third in South Africa, fourth in New York, and last in Canada. Domino wrote a recommendation letter to include with each.

Then I dove into financial-aid possibilities—grants and scholarships—realizing paying for this on my own was definitely doable. Cade was right. I didn't need my parents' money. I could and would do this. And that thought made me so proud.

"Hey, sis, whatcha smiling about?" Frederick asked, entering the room.

Sis. I loved hearing Frederick say that. "Just thinking about my future."

Frederick glanced across the living room to the chessboard. "Up for a game?"

"Sure." I put my paperwork aside and headed over.

"Heard back from your letter home yet?" Frederick asked as we set up the board.

"No." It upset me more than I wanted to admit. It wasn't like I expected an immediate phone call, but the total lack of response shocked me.

"Not even Gwenny?"

I shook my head, definitely concerned about my sister. I'd texted her a few times, but got nothing back. I could only imagine what was going on.

Frederick pushed a pawn out. "And Cade?"

I sighed. "I haven't heard from him, either."

"You still mad at him?"

I took a knight up and over. "No. In fact, I don't think I ever really was. I can understand he was trying to respect everyone's privacy. Personally, I would have hated to be in his shoes, knowing something so huge."

Frederick slid his bishop three diagonal spaces. "I hope he comes back soon, wherever he is."

"Yeah, I miss him," I admitted.

"Me too."

I slid a pawn left and took out his bishop.

Frederick studied the board for a second, obviously perplexed as to how I had just captured his man.

As he pondered his next move, Tilly strolled in. "Frederick, honey, will you please go help Beth? She's trying to get Cottage One ready for some last-minute guests."

Frederick pushed back from the chess table. "Sure."

"Want me to help too?" I asked.

Tilly shooed Frederick away. "No."

I watched my brother stride off before turning my attention back to Tilly. "I'm glad you two are back to normal."

She smiled. "Me too," she said, and sat down in the chair he'd vacated. "We've been invited to the art gallery for an opening tomorrow. Do you want to come?"

I brightened. "Definitely!"

"Good. I'll RSVP, then." Tilly got up. She stood for a second staring down at me, and I got the impression she wanted to say something but didn't know how to say it. "Em . . . don't make the same mistake I did. Don't leave them behind. Continue to write them, call them, show them you care. They may not respond, but you can rise above them. You're a bigger and better person for taking the initiative. Understand what I'm saying?"

I nodded. "I do. I definitely plan to keep trying even if they try to freeze me out."

Tilly winked. "Good."

I sighed. "I'm worried about Gwenny more than anything."

"She'll be fine. You two will always be sisters. Nothing can or will come between you two."

Tilly was right. Nothing had ever come between Gwenny

and me, and we certainly wouldn't let this.

"I'm glad you're here, Em. I'm glad you decided to stay."

I laughed a little. "I never even officially asked you if I *could* stay. I just assumed . . ."

Tilly waved me off. "You assumed right. I can't think of anything better."

And neither could I.

* * *

That night I wrote another letter. I promised myself I would write home once a week and follow up with a call. I was starting to doubt they would respond, but I knew it was the right thing to do. I didn't want to lose contact with the only family I'd known for seventeen years. Eventually, I'd wear them down. Eventually.

The next morning Gwenny called.

"Gwenny! Where have you been? I've been going nuts over here. Didn't you get my texts?"

My sister sighed. "They took my phone away. They didn't want me calling you. They don't want us talking."

"Oh, Gwenny." I so didn't want them taking all this out on her.

"I know. It sucks. But get this, Dad stepped in on our behalf."

"Get out!" Dad *never* overrode Mom and Grandmother.

"He said that it was very mean-spirited to keep the two of us from talking."

"He said 'mean-spirited'?" I couldn't imagine.

"That's right."

"Wow. So, how is everyone taking it?"

"Well, the first couple of days were really bad. Grandmother and Mom even discussed flying down there and confronting you."

I swallowed. "They're not, are they?"

"No. And of course they wanted to know what I knew."

"I'm sorry, Gwenny. I never meant to put you in the middle."

"Whatever. And now they're just real silent. Grandmother's telling everyone you're taking a year off to volunteer with underprivileged orphans."

"Doesn't surprise me. She's so about image it's ridiculous. Is it really so horrible that I want to go to culinary school?"

"Oh, you know how she is. So the way I figure it, we need to give them some time. You write another letter. And I'll work on them here. Now that Dad seems to be on our side, I'm going to get him wearing them down too."

And she would. My sister could be very convincing when she set her mind to it. She's the one who should be a lawyer.

We said our good-byes and I headed downstairs to help Domino with breakfast. He was all set in the kitchen, so I helped Tilly serve the guests.

Harry, the yacht man, greeted me when I came out with the first tray of food. "Good morning."

I smiled and laid a plate down in front of him. "I'm surprised to see you here. Is your boat still being repaired?"

"Oh, I'm back living on it now, but your aunt lets me come

and eat whenever I want to. I've become quite a fan of the food here."

I refilled his coffee, then paused. "Mr. Lemley, if you don't mind me asking, do I know you from somewhere? Your name sounds very familiar."

He smiled mysteriously. "No, I don't think we know each other."

"Hm." I studied him. "Well, enjoy your breakfast."

* * *

That night we headed downtown to the opening at the art gallery.

We strolled along the cobblestone street, passing all the unique shops, some open and some closed for the evening. We crossed in front of the glass-blowing shop and I glanced down the alley toward the door that led to Cade's apartment, wishing he was with me.

As we neared the gallery, guitar music filtered through the air, soft and dreamy. People spilled out of the gallery and into the stone entryway.

Beth stood in the crowd, and I spotted Jeremy, too. He gave me a friendly wave and a smile, and I waved back. We hadn't seen or talked to each other since the phone call when he broke up with me. I'd thought things would be awkward, but they weren't at all.

Jeremy really was a nice guy; he just wasn't the right guy for me.

I followed Tilly and Frederick under the arched entryway

and into the gallery. I recognized many of the faces around me, and they recognized me, too, with friendly hellos and waves.

I felt right at home. I felt like a local.

As I wove my way through the gallery, I began looking at the paintings on display. There was one of the cemetery where Cade's mom was buried. Another of the cave Cade had taken me to on our first date. One of a small plane flying over the ocean. One of a figure that looked like Domino swinging in a hammock.

I recognized the work—it was by the same person who had done all the other ones I had seen hanging around the island and in the Pepper House.

I remembered the first few that I had seen. I'd wanted to climb right into every one of them and their wonderful whirl of lifelike colors.

I came to the last one, a picture of a gorgeous dark-haired woman sunbathing in a black-and-gold bikini on the beach. She had her eyes closed as the sun tanned her already golden skin. Her long wavy hair stretched out behind her, making trails in the sand.

She was beautiful.

I leaned in for a closer look and immediately sucked in a breath as realization dawned.

The figure in the painting was *me*!

"What do you think?"

I whipped around. "Cade? Where have you been?"

He didn't answer me and instead shook his head. "I'm sorry, Em."

"What. . . ."

He looked down at the floor. "I've thought it all through and I realize I should have said something. I shouldn't have kept such a big secret from you."

I took his hand, once again feeling the connection between us. "No," I told him. "Absolutely not. It wasn't your secret to tell."

Cade brought his eyes up to me. "You're not upset?"

My heart turned over with tenderness. "I was. But I'm not anymore."

"Thanks."

We stood there for a few seconds, holding hands, and finally his mouth tilted up in that sexy little half-grin. Then he pulled me in for a warm hug.

I squeezed him back. "I missed you. Where have you been?"

He pressed a soft kiss to my cheek. "On the mainland."

"The mainland? What were you doing there?"

Cade shrugged. "This and that."

"Well, that's very mysterious."

He laughed a little. "And I missed you, too. I guess you being here means you're staying?"

"For a while, anyway. I'm applying to culinary schools."

"Em." Cade tugged me in for another quick hug. "That's awesome."

We stood there smiling, staring at each other. I let myself get lost in his tender blue eyes, when a voice called out, "Ladies and gentlemen, may I have your attention?"

Everyone got quiet and we turned our attention to the

owner of the gallery. She motioned around the room. "I want to thank everybody for coming. Tonight is very special for us. For years you have all seen these paintings hanging around the island. Many of you have asked who the artist is, and unfortunately, I haven't been permitted to say.

"This artist is a local," she continued. "He began painting about five years ago, when he was still just a boy. I recognized talent in him from the start. Neither one of us realized the extent to which his paintings would take off. We sold his first painting about three years ago. Then another. And another.

"I'm happy to announce that this week he officially went international. We sold a painting to a buyer in England, another in Japan, and two more in Australia. This artist isn't one for public speeches, but we do want to acknowledge him. So"—the gallery owner lifted her champagne glass—"let's all give a toast to Cade Farrell, our resident artist."

A hush fell over the crowd.

I rewound her last statement in my brain. *Cade?*

One person started to clap, followed by another, and another.

Soon the entire room filled with celebratory cheers and applause.

I barely heard any of it as I stood beside Cade, completely shocked.

Gradually, people began coming over to offer congratulations. The crowd around him grew, edging me away. I turned a slow circle, taking in all the paintings, some depicting scenes from his own life. How could I have not known something so huge? How could I not have realized?

My gaze came to rest on the image of the sunbathing woman.

"Straight from my imagination," Cade said from behind me. "Beth told me you had a hot black-and-gold bikini."

I blushed. "I don't look this good in it."

"Well, you'll just have to model it for me and let me decide that."

I blushed even more. "I can't believe *you're* the artist."

Cade smiled a little.

I ran my gaze around the room again, over all the paintings, barely noting all the people standing around us. "Do you know how many of these I've seen this summer? I've been mesmerized by these paintings and *you're* the artist. It's unbelievable." I brought my eyes to rest on him. "And you're *amazing*," I added softly.

Cade actually looked embarrassed. "Thanks."

"How many people knew?"

He gave a guilty shrug. "Only Tilly and Carol, the woman who owns this gallery. Actually, Tilly is the person who brought me here when she saw me sketching one day."

I stared at Cade, trying to comprehend it all. And to think I'd thought he was a loser the first time I met him. He was anything but.

Cade's brows lifted. "Say something?"

"I'm . . . I'm so proud of you." I closed the small distance between us and gave him a huge hug.

He hugged me back. "Thanks."

"Cade," the gallery owner interrupted us. "There are a few people I'd like you to meet."

Cade pressed a kiss to my cheek. "Meet me afterward?"

"Definitely."

* * *

After the party, Cade and I strolled down Key Street.

I squeezed his hand. "Frederick couldn't stop talking about you the whole night. He pretended like he knew all along."

Cade laughed. "I hope he's not too upset I didn't let him in on my little secret."

"No, he's fine. And you two talked about the other big secret?"

Cade nodded.

We continued walking, holding hands, enjoying the peacefulness of the night.

In the shadows of a huge tree, Cade pulled me aside and gave me the most tender, slow, loving kiss. While we'd kissed before, there was something special about this one, something deeper. Like our relationship had just moved to yet another level. I knew so much more about Cade, and myself, and it felt wonderful.

After a moment, Cade pulled back a little to look me in the eye. "I'm really happy that you're here, that you're staying."

"Me too."

He looked down at our joined hands. "I've thought about you nearly every second over the past week. I missed you."

My heart swelled with emotion. Lifting our hands, I kissed his. "I've missed you, too."

Letting out a shaky breath, he looked me in the eye. "I've . . .

I've never felt this way about anybody before."

I smiled at his sweet admission, and as I stared into his gorgeous eyes, my heart began to pound. "Cade . . ."

He took a step back, studying my face. "What's wrong?"

I sighed. "It's just . . . I'm here now, but I'll be leaving soon. I'm hoping to get into a January culinary class."

Cade took my hand. "Em, there's no place around here to study cooking and you can't just apprentice under Domino. I know all that. We'll figure it out. I'm not going anywhere."

I stepped into his arms and we shared a long hug. "So are you going to tell me why you missed me?" I teased.

"Why do girls always have to know more?" he joked, and I laughed. "OK, for starters your food."

"Cade!"

He chuckled and, taking my hand, he led me from the shadows back down Key Street. "Then there's that sense of adventure you have hidden deep inside. And the beauty you have outside," he said, and I blushed. "The love you have for your family. But most importantly, your bravery."

"Bravery?"

"Em, you learned some pretty surprising news this summer and not a lot of people would've have handled it as bravely as you did."

I thought about that for a few seconds and realized it *had* taken bravery and guts for me to tackle my family secret, step forward, and take the opportunity to be the person I knew I wanted to be. Hearing Cade say it brought me a true sense of satisfaction.

Things made so much more sense now. Growing up and feeling stifled. Coming here and sensing an immediate connection. This place really was home for me. This was what I had been missing in my life, and I hadn't even known it.

Cade squeezed my hand, bringing me out of my thoughts. "You going to tell me why you missed me?"

"Why do boys always have to know more?" I joked, and he laughed at my mimicry.

I smiled. "Your sense of humor, for one. The deepness in your heart that you don't let many people see. The love you have for this island and the people who live here. Your dedication to the Pepper House. The way you challenge me to step out of the norm. Your sense of freedom and independence." I touched the ring he always wore around his neck. "And the fact that you always wear this."

He gave me a sexy grin. "That's quite a list. I think you did better than me."

"That's OK," I teased. "You can expand on yours anytime."

Loving someone so much that you're lost in him. Those were words I had been thinking about a lot lately. I couldn't have imagined that feeling back at the beginning of the summer, and now . . . I could.

Epilogue

More than a month had gone by since that night at the art show. It was September. Every week I wrote and left a message on the home machine and every week was the same: no response. Gwenny and I talked every few days, thankfully, but I was really disappointed with my parents.

I was also still waiting to hear back from the culinary schools I'd applied to.

In the meantime, Cade and I were doing great. Wonderful, in fact. We had reached such a level of understanding and respect, it was if we had known each other for years rather than just months.

Things were normal around the Pepper House. I would get up early and help Domino cook, then assist Beth in the afternoons since Frederick had started back to school.

Cade was in and out doing his thing. At night he and I would hang out at his place or somewhere else around the island. My life was so different from the way it had been, more different than I ever could have imagined. But it felt wonderful. I could finally breathe and be myself.

I was standing in the kitchen with Domino, kneading dough for a scrumptious papaya pie. As I had admitted before, dessert cooking was not my forte.

"Em?"

I glanced over at Domino. "Yeah?"

"We"—he nodded at Tilly, who was standing on the other side of the kitchen island sipping cranberry juice—"have been hiding something from you."

I looked between them. "Oh?" My stomach balled up—not another secret.

"You know Harry?" Tilly asked.

"The guy from the yacht?" I asked slowly. "Yeah, actually, I've been completely puzzled by him. His name sounds so familiar."

Domino nodded. "Harold Lemley. Put on your culinary hat, Em. *The* Harold Lemley . . ."

I ran that name around in my head . . . "*The* Harold Lemley?" I repeated, realization slowly settling in. "Oh my God."

Domino grinned.

"How long have you two known?"

Domino cringed. "Since about the second week he was here."

"I can't believe it!" I picked the dough up I'd been kneading and threw it back into the bowl. "I've been cooking for *the* Harold Lemley? Food critic Harold Lemley?" Immediately, I began recalling all the things I'd made that he'd eaten. All the things I could have done differently. All the mistakes I'd made.

I paced away from the bowl. "I put Bisquick in yesterday's sausage balls. I would *never* have used Bisquick if I'd known *Harold Lemley* was eating them!"

Tilly held her hands up, laughing. "Calm down. There's more."

I turned to both of them. "What do you mean there's more?"

"He wants to have a meeting with you," Domino said.

"What?!" I looked between them, my heart racing. "Why?"

"He was impressed with you from day one," Tilly told me. "And when he found out about your cooking aspirations and applications to culinary schools, he offered to write you a personal recommendation."

My jaw dropped. "He did not."

Domino smiled. "He did. And there's still more."

"I don't know if I can take any more."

Tilly grinned. "He's sponsoring a scholarship to one well-deserving student, and he wants you to apply for it. It'll pay for tuition, room, and board at a school of your choice."

I screamed and threw myself into Tilly's arms. "HAROLD LEMLEY!" I screamed again.

She laughed. "We've scheduled a meeting for this afternoon for you two to discuss it all."

"Oh." I turned in a circle. "I need to make a list. I need to do some research. What will I say to him? What should I wear?"

They both laughed at me.

"Go!" They shooed me away.

* * *

That afternoon I drove the van to the marina, where Harold Lemley's yacht was tied off. Wearing a simple coral skirt and a white blouse, I strode down the dock toward the end. As I neared Sid's spot, I glanced over to see him sitting beneath the canopy, with Cade beside him.

I waved hello, trying not to show my surprise at seeing Cade there.

Cade jumped off the boat and trotted over to me. "You look nice."

I turned my back so Sid couldn't see me ask, "What are you doing? Is everything OK?"

Cade smiled. "Yeah, it's getting there."

"How long have you been talking to Sid?"

"A couple of days now." Cade shrugged. "You inspired me, Em, dealing with your family, still trying with them even though they're giving you the cold shoulder." He took my hand. "I took the initiative to talk to Sid. It's not perfect, but it's a start."

I smiled. "I'm glad."

We stood there, holding hands, looking at each other. I didn't think I could be more proud of Cade than I was at that moment.

He looked me up and down. "Why are you so dressed up?"

I told him all about my impending meeting with Harold Lemley.

"Em!" Cade grabbed me up and swung me around. "That's great!"

"I know." I straightened my outfit and gave him a quick kiss. "I've got to get to my meeting."

"Go!" he said, shooing me off just like Tilly and Domino had.

I walked over to the yacht and boarded.

"Em," Mr. Lemley greeted me. "It's so nice to see you. Come, sit down."

We sat outside on the upper deck of his yacht. I wasn't nearly as nervous as I thought I'd be. We talked about cooking, of course, and he described what culinary school was like, what I could expect out of each day, and how hard I would be expected to work.

He advised me to explore as much as possible. We discussed techniques, theories, and cuisine. He encouraged me to experiment as much Domino would allow.

Harold and I spoke about opportunities afterward, once I'd earned my degree, but I told him what I'd put on all my applications—I could think of nothing better than staying right here and opening my own restaurant.

Toward the end of our hour-long conversation, he assured me he would write a recommendation letter to each of the five schools I had applied to. And he officially offered me the scholarship he was sponsoring. Of course, I happily accepted.

Now I just had to wait to hear back from the culinary institutions.

* * *

"Guess what?!" I told Gwenny two weeks later.

"What?"

"I got into all five schools!"

She screamed. "Oh, Em, I'm so proud of you!"

"Thanks!"

"So which one are you going to chose?"

"Italy."

Gwenny sighed. "Oh, that sounds so romantic. Can I come visit you and maybe meet a hot Italian guy?"

I laughed. "Definitely."

"What about Cade?"

"The thought of leaving him is killing me. But he's been great about everything. I'll come back here during holidays. And he's actually going to be doing some gallery shows, so he'll be in Italy two times that he knows of already. I can't wait to be there with him!"

"I want your life."

I smiled. *My life.* I felt as though it had finally begun.

"Yesterday Mom asked me if your letter had arrived yet," Gwenny went on.

My heart skipped a beat of excitement. "Really?"

"I think that's progress. She used to pretend indifference. I think she's softening."

I sighed.

"Listen, I've got to run. Say hi to everybody."

"Will do." I pressed End and got my paper and pen. I couldn't wait to write home. I had so much to share—and now I knew my mom was looking for the letter.

* * *

December rolled around. I had continued my weekly letters and calls home. The last week of November I finally received a response. It was just a short note from my mom:

> Elizabeth Margaret, we would like to accept your
> invitation to spend Christmas with you in the Outer
> Banks.
> Thank you. You can expect Gwyneth, your dad, and your
> grandmother, and me.
> We will see you December 23rd.
> With love, Mom

I gripped that note in my hand as I stood outside of the airport waiting for them to exit baggage claim. Frederick was with me, along with Tilly and, of course, Cade. In my head, I'd played this scene out lots of times and hoped for the absolute best.

"This is all because of you," Tilly whispered.

Smiling at that thought, I looked over at Cade, feeling the nerves rustling around in my stomach. He gave me a cute wink that calmed me.

Gwenny came out of baggage claim came first. She took one look at me and bolted across the pavement to where I stood. We hugged and laughed and started to cry.

My mom, dad, and grandmother followed. They all stood in a line studying us as we stood studying them. It was like there was this invisible barrier neither side wanted to cross.

I made the first move.

I went to my mom, not even bothering to hide the tears in my eyes, and gave her a welcoming hug. "I missed you, Mom."

She sniffed. "I missed you, too."

Dad stepped forward and hugged me next. "You look great, sweetheart."

I kissed his cheek. "Thanks, Dad."

Grandmother stood a little behind them staring across the space at Tilly.

Everyone quietly watched as Tilly closed the gap between them and came to stand right in front of my grandmother. "Mother," she said simply.

Grandmother's bottom lip trembled and it made fresh tears fall from my eyes. I'd never seen my grandmother show any emotion other than haughtiness.

Tilly gave Grandmother a tentative hug that slowly grew into something more familiar and warm.

I introduced Frederick to my New England family and Gwenny to my island family.

Tilly took my mom's hand. "Thank you for raising such a fabulous daughter, Kat."

My mom nodded, trying to hold back emotion, and gave her younger sister a hug.

I stood watching everyone make the first steps to healing,

the first strides to bandaging up our family, and thought, I did this. Me. I brought all these wonderful people back together.

Cade carefully approached, and I introduced him around.

While my family stood talking, Cade leaned over and whispered into my ear, "I love you, Elizabeth Margaret. You're amazing."

His words sank into my soul. I thought of the girl I was when I first arrived—a little scared and at the same time excited. I thought of the woman I had become, free and happy and completely comfortable with myself. I thought of my future as a chef and how all my dreams had come true. I thought of my family, of Cade, and falling in love.

He was right; I *was* amazing.